The Year They CANCELED CHRISTMAS

THE YEAR THEY CANCELED CHRISTMAS

STORIES

JAMES D. MCCALLISTER

Mind Harvest Press
COLUMBIA, SC

ISBN: 978-1-946052-02-5

Library of Congress Control Number: 2017914433

For more information:

Mind Harvest Press
C O L U M B I A , S C

Mind Harvest Press
PO Box 50552
Columbia SC 29250-0552
www.mindharvestpress.com
www.jamesdmccallister.com

A narrative is like a room on whose walls a number of false doors have been painted; while within the narrative, we have many apparent choices of exit, but when the author leads us to one particular door, we know it is the right one because it opens.

JOHN UPDIKE

CONTENTS

Benj struggles with the ten-by-ten white lawn-tent while Marcy goes through the beads, box by box: Disco Ball Throw Beads, Tumblin' Dice Throw Beads, Heart Shaped Throw Beads, Oversize Mardi Gras Specials (they look like a necklace of round, green Christmas ornaments, and take up so much space that Marcy wants to scream), Peace Sign Throw Beads, Mystic Leaf Throw Beads (which are pot leaves, in about six colors, including bling-bling gold and silver), Spurting Penis Throw Beads (a new addition), Kiss Me I'm Irish Green Shamrock Throw Beads (leftover from the St. Pat's Festival in Savannah), and a giant blue tub of just ordinary old Throw Beads, which at two for a dollar are a big money generator in spite of their comparative simplicity. That tub is the one that both of them hate the most; seasoned festival vendors they might be, but it didn't make the boxes and storage bins of colorful, plastic junk any lighter—especially after all these years on the road.

They'd gotten up at the crack of dawn and had a big breakfast at the Waffle House—or Awful House, as Benj calls it—next to the Highway Rest Express motel. Another lousy meal at another cruddy roadside diner, one of a thousand such breakfasts that all run together into a fatty stew of heavy omelets, greasy burgers, salty fries that taste of the old oil in which they've been scalded, Cobb salads of yellow, tasteless iceberg lettuce and mealy tomatoes, eggs on the side of steaks as tough as shoe leather, weak iced tea with a hair in it, burned, bitter restaurant coffee, half-thawed frozen meringue pie on a cracked plate, and then maybe a cig or two (even they're both trying to cut back). They've lived this way so long it just seems natural, somehow.

Benj finds himself belching his hashbrowns-smothered-with-onions as they make their way onto the festival grounds and all during the setup, but rushing through another crappy breakfast has paid off: With a double sawbuck, they grease the palm of the sleepy-eyed festival intern who is assigning the spots, and she pencils them into a prime corner location near the end of the food vendors, only forty yards from the main music stage. They'll be deaf by the end of the day, but that is the price you pay in their line for having prime real estate in a high foot-traffic area. If only his back didn't hurt so much; if only the indigestion deigns to succumb to the Zantac 150's that he will gobble off and on all day; if only her feet hold out; if only they can sell some stuff—not just cover the vendor fee, but *make some money*. If only, if only.

The neighbors arrive—they are a couple of guys, Steve and Earl, who sell stickers (three bucks each or two for five) from wall-size Plexiglas displays that they set up in rows and hang from poles that they stick into the ground if it is dirt like the vendor areas thankfully are at this festival. The sticker dudes are on a first name basis with Benj and Marcy from prior encounters, and since Benj and Marcy don't sell stickers, Steve and Earl are always real friendly and cooperative. The four vendors exchange pleasantries and then get back to work.

Soon Marcy and Benj then find themselves more or less set up and ready for business, so he leaves for a few minutes—it's barely ten in the morning, and the music doesn't start until noon—to get in a quick potty-break before the early-bird customers start wandering onto the sprawling festival site. Laid out over the state fairgrounds just outside of town, the festival area shares a huge parking lot with the local college football stadium, so there is plenty of room for thousands of would-be festival attendees. Benj is optimistic. The weather is beautiful, and for a minute, as he smells the food wagons getting ready and shuffles through the sawdust and the hay scattered around, he remembers how much he used to enjoy this work.

The portajohns, a line of which stretches for fifty yards, stand in formation like a platoon of stolid, sea-foam green soldiers at attention, ready for duty; at this early hour they are as fresh and pristine as they will be all day. Benj sits quietly and thumbs through a Tom Robbins paperback he's already read while he waits for something to happen. He has a wispy corona of long hair surrounding an expansive bald pate, the mostly-salt and pepper locks pulled back into a short ponytail. His ass is getting as big as the side of a house, as his grandmother would have said; he is no spring chicken. His back hurts and his bad knee hurts and his hip—old man's hip, Marcy calls it only half-jokingly—is really acting up today. He knows this life is too hard on him, he knows he should lose some weight, he knows that sometimes he's not sure how happy he is, he knows that his choices are limited. This is some life I've carved out for myself, he thinks. And the festival season, stretching on into the autumn, is only beginning.

But this is how we make our living—everybody's gotta do something.

He's mildly surprised that they're even working this particular event again; last year, the struggling music festival had been declared by the city council to be all but moribund, until a last minute grassroots petition campaign convinced the municipality to underwrite the shortfall—again—and give the organizers one last shot to make it into the black. The city had wanted the music festival in the first place as a badge of honor, as a prestige, tourist-attracting feather in its cap, but all it has turned out to be is a bit of a joke around town.

And so this year the organizers have done all they can to achieve success: slightly reduced admission, a wide-ranging roster of acts, a kiddie-fair with rides, loads of advertising, even more vendors of both food and souvenirs. Benj has heard that advance ticket sales have apparently been brisk, but you know how people talk a good game. Still—the day should be good.

A number of musical genres are represented, with the two biggest acts being a goth-makeup-metal group called Outflank, who'll be headlining the main stage just across from Benj and Marcy's tent. At the other end of the long strip of tarmac is a stage featuring hip-hop trio Blingo, currently enjoying their fifteen seconds of fame on the pop charts after winning a television talent contest. Side stages will feature other talent of varying stature. Benj hopes against hope that the two main crowds, as different in temperament and taste as night and day, won't intermingle with unsettling results. These festivals are always a challenge, especially as the day of beer drinking and carousing lengthens into evening; a mini-riot is the last thing anyone wants. With kids today, though, you just don't ever know.

Benj frets and rubs his bad knee and cleans himself and then struggles to squeeze his enormous backside out of the now-soiled porta-john, its pine-scented freshness irrevocably lost. Benj feels tired already. And only fourteen hours of work ahead—that is, if the breakdown later tonight goes quickly.

Marcy is yawning and setting up the grid panels on which they will display the novelty shirts: the pothead and beer drinking joke-shirts, the tie-dyes (the sign spells it "tye-dyes" however), the left-over St Pat's shirts from Savannah. "I'll get those, hon," Benj offers good-naturedly; he knows Marcy's back hurts too, and those seven-foot grids are unwieldy bastards.

"I'll put out the jewelry, then."

"And the hats," Benj reminds gently.

"I know," she says with a sad smile. "Want some coffee?" She produces the thermos they filled up out of the complimentary decanters in the motel lobby.

"Not yet, babe," he mutters through an acid belch.

∼

IT'S A SLOW-STARTER, this festival, which isn't all that unusual. Benj listens to a ball game while Marcy reads. They've both smoked three cigarettes already, in direct violation of their pact to only smoke that many all day.

Two o'clock rolls around; the sun is no longer baking them. All the stages are live, now, at least, and there's some traffic but nothing about which to write home. The supporting acts are a motley mix of local bands, the ones everyone sees all month long around town—every month!—and a couple of seventies warhorses—Kansas, with one original member, and Styx, with two—but that's about it. The fairgrounds are dotted only by a few hundred people milling around, most of whom look too much like Benj and Marcy to want much of what they sell, which is aimed at a younger, drunker crowd. Sales are non-existent for hours, it seems; the first one of note is a "tye-dye" shirt to a fifty-something guy who regales them for fifteen minutes (after squinting and whining about the price of the shirt, begging for an "old timer's discount, heh heh") about the time he saw Janis Joplin and how he remembers the way he felt when he heard she'd died, and about Hendrix, and about how he didn't get into the Doors at all until after Morrison died, but then he thought they were just, just, just the most profound of them all, the Doors. "That shit's like poetry, and shit, man. Y'know? Dang."

"I know," Benj replies. "Did you know they were all twenty-seven?"

"Who?"

"All of 'em. Jimi, Janis, Jim . . . Brian Jones. Pigpen, from the Grateful Dead. Even Kurt Cobain . . ."

Marcy smiles as Benj produces the "Forever 27" T-shirt with a flourish from a bin under the jewelry table. The artwork features a ghostly Kurt Cobain entering a bar—a bar called heaven—as the other dead rock stars sit strumming instruments, all of them save Pigpen—a scowling, tough, blues-biker of a figure, as in life—sporting beatific, angelic expressions on their faces. "Isn't that something," Benj says, more of a statement than a question. "Mm-hm," he continues, reverent.

"Dude," the so-called old timer asks, misty-eyed, "tell me you got one a them in a two-X." Benj turns and winks at Marcy as he digs one out of the bin.

BENJ YAWNS. Marcy sips the old coffee and wrinkles her nose. They sell stuff here and there, two dollars, five dollars, ten dollars worth of throw beads to a drunk guy who already has twenty dollars' worth around his neck.

"Stir fry?" Marcy looks over at Benj and gives him an exaggerated, I'm-hungry belly rub.

"I want a gyro, I think."

"Ugh," Marcy says.

"Nah," Benj jokes. "That tzatziki sauce, it's good for you. Mmmmm." And now he too does the belly rub. If he's made it once, he's made the joke a thousand times.

BENJ'S HEAD is pounding as the opener for Outflank is tuning up —not playing, mind you, just tuning up—but at least sales have picked up, finally, in the last hour or so. Marcy's frowning as she eagle-eyes some kids pawing through the basket of hacky sacks while an accomplice thinks he is discreetly fingering the display of Indian incense boxes (some of it so old that it probably just smells like a burning twig now). The incense comes in narrow, square ten-stick boxes that go for only a buck apiece, and she thinks *why don't you just fucking buy one, you cheap little bastard, instead of trying to wait me out and take one* as her own headache begins slowly pulsing into existence behind her eyes.

Finally Benj waddles over and stands there with a sour expression, glowering down at the three little punks with their long bangs died different colors and their oily looking jeans and t-shirts for bands that were stars before the wearers were even born. After a long frustrating minute for both the vendors and the would-be boosters, the boys give up and move on just as a longhair biker type starts asking if they have any glass pieces and his girlfriend engages Marcy about the toe rings and the throw beads and the scented oils. Benj motions the guy over to the side of the tent, where he opens a padded case full of hand-blown, colorful glass "tobacco" pipes that are shown out of sight at this festival since it is a conservative town. Following a genial negotiation, he sells the guy a small bubbler for sixty bucks, after coming off the original price quote of seventy-five (which still makes Benj his keystone markup anyway). He gives the biker a small packet of tobacco in case the guy's a narc. He concludes the transaction with a grateful wink as he hands the three crisp twenties to Marcy, who stashes them in her hip pack, which functions as the cash register. The bubbler is the biggest sale of the day, other than the two t-shirts to the weepy nostalgia-suffused customer from earlier.

SURE ENOUGH, sometime around eight o'clock, a fight breaks out not too far from the tent, right in the middle of the sticker-guys' setup next door. And sure enough, it's between some gangsta types there for Blingo and some greasy white redneck-metal looking kids. The white kids sport a combination of wallet chains, black clothing, oversize pants, ball caps, and bad skin. The black guys, in oversized athletic gear and huge t-shirts featuring icons such as Tupac and Marley, are trying to play it cool but the big fat redneck guy is shiny-eyed and yelling about someone pulling on his wallet chain and then he's sticking his finger in one guy's face, after which one of the black dudes starts yelling about *ain't no moth-erfucker gon' pull yo' chain, niggah,* and then the blows start flying and one of the acrylic sticker-boards, as tall as a man, falls over in a tangle of bodies but then the cops show, and it breaks up fast as the principals are hauled aside while their accomplices melt away into the gathering throng.

Marcy looks pained and stressed, her head pounding, and tells Benj it looks like someone has taken a display t-shirt while she had her back turned watching the fight but before he can respond the three little assholes are back fingering the hackey-sacks and incense again and someone walks up and asks how much the spurting-penis throw beads are just as Outflank kicks into their opening number *AT A VOLUME THAT IS SO EAR-SPLIT-TINGLY DISTORTED* that Benj bites his tongue hard enough to make it bleed and tears squirt out of his eyes when he tries to choke out, "Three dollars, or two for five."

Marcy has shoved cotton into her ears and is standing with her arms folded watching people stream by without so much as a glance at any of the merch. People are pumping their fists in the air to the heavy beat and throwing beer at each other. Benj has already packed some merch away into the bins even though it is only ten o'clock—beads have sold for shit, and it takes so long to put all that stuff away that he just can't stand the thought of having to do it afterwards, even though he knows sometimes this is the time of the night when you can sell it by the handful to all the drunks. But it's the beginning of the season, after all, and they haven't done too badly today. The hip pack around Marcy's ample waist is fairly bulging with bills—although most of them are ones, of course. But it adds up, sometimes. People would be surprised, Benj thinks. Not with today's take, but on a really good weekend . . . ?

But there haven't been that many of those in the last year or two, and for all kinds of reasons: Competition, declining atten-dance—it all costs so much these days, from the tickets to the parking to the corndogs to the, yes, souvenirs, the tchotchkes and crap that Marcy and Benj sell. Not to mention the difficulty in programming festivals in the first place, with the fractured, fragmented, compartmentalized, sub-genred-to-death music business such as it is—not to mention the overabundance of the festivals themselves, which they have these days for every reason from celebrating bluegrass to jam bands to nostalgia, to diversity or unity or a combination thereof, to okra or crawfish, or else to spring time or harvest time, to Chinese New Year's and Arbor Day, to the fourth of July and Easter Sunday and Fat Tuesday, to ones like this one which just sort of *are* for their own sake. And with all the choices that people have nowadays—hell, with five or six hundred TV channels who needs to leave the house anyway?—Benj is surprised that people like he and Marcy—his love, his sweet girl, always at his side—can still make a living doing what they do. On the other hand, people will probably always need a reason to get outside and drink beer and congregate in cliques and groups and families, and hopefully in the process leave a little money behind. Benj thinks sometimes that he'll keel over at one of these damn festivals; "just step over me on the way out," he always says.

"Why don't we open a brick-and-mortar somewhere," Marcy says as she grunts a bin into the back of the van. The music's over, the cops are pushing all the drunks out in the parking lot, the moon is up and the area in front of the stage is a sea of garbage. "A college town. Or at the beach. Work the season, hang out in the winter time . . ."

"That's what we do now."

"But I mean stay in one place. Think about it, baby. Somewhere warm all winter, the Carolinas. Myrtle Beach. St. Simon's Island. Florida—Panama City or Lauderdale or the Keys, baby, the *Keys*—"

Benj goes over and puts his hands on her shoulders. "That'd take some mad cash, girlfriend. You got some I ain't heard about?" Benj says this half-wishing that she does.

"I don't, unfortunately. Just this." She fingers the hip-pack and shrugs.

"Lot of us there already," he says, continuing to play devil's advocate, thinking of all the established head shops and jewelry huts and airbrush guys and souvenir vendors in a place like Myrtle Beach. "Tough to make a go of it. Long hours." Benj had worked retail as a teenager and hated it. "Lot of the same problems. Hard work," he concludes.

"And this ain't?"

Benj kisses her on top of the head. "No one said it'd be easy. Least not—"

"—to me, anyway," finishing one of Benj's familiar bromides. "We're getting too old for this mess, hon," she adds with one of her own.

His knee hurts and his hip flares and his back twinges. "Don't have to tell me."

"So what are we going to do?"

Benj laughs and starts sliding the grid panels into their space inside the van. "Work the season, work the circuit, get through the year. Who knows? Maybe it'll be an up year. Maybe—maybe by the end of the summer we'll be all set."

"All set?"

Benj stops and looks at her. "You know what I mean."

"Yeah, right," she scoffs. "Ah, well." Marcy turns and stoops over to drag a cardboard box of t-shirts over toward the van. "Help me with this, hon."

"You got it, babe." In another few minutes the tent comes down and the van is loaded and they say goodbye to the sticker guys, who ask if they did all right. Benj looks forward to a late night snack back to the motel; Marcy wants to smoke a joint and have a soak in the bath. They don't have to get up early in the morning, so why not, she thinks.

The morning brings the drive back home, where upon their arrival they will check their various E-bay auctions and get together whatever items need to be shipped out. Then they will restock the road merch before heading out to work the Magnolia Music Fest next weekend, two hundred miles in the opposite direction, three days' worth of the same-old routine. Outflank is playing again one of the nights, unfortunately, but so is one of the Grateful Dead members who is still touring around, and Benj is kind of looking forward to that one, for once, along with Buddy Guy on another stage and Aretha Franklin on still another. Benj will not make it over to watch any of those legends though—but then again he's not there for the music anyway. Not really.

He thinks that, back home, he will go online and look at real estate and businesses for sale in resort towns like Marcy was talking about; he won't say anything about it to her, though—they don't have the money to do much of anything but buy some more merch to sell this season, so why get her hopes up? Doesn't hurt to dream, he thinks. And she's right about one thing—too old for this shit. Besides—maybe some amazing deal is just waiting out there to be found. Maybe they'll fall ass-backwards into a stake of some undetermined amount.

Maybe they'll hit the Lotto. You never know about things. Just keep plugging away until it happens—that is what Benj thinks as he signals and changes lanes and then pulls off into the motel parking lot.

In the light of day again, the beads shake and the grids rattle as the van rumbles down the interstate. Marcy reaches over and holds Benj's hand, who smiles at her even though his hip is killing him. We enjoy our freedom, he thinks. We are beholden to no one but each other—and our customers, of course. She counts the money from yesterday, writes some numbers in a ledger book that they keep, and looks out at the countryside rolling by while Benj sings along to an old song on the radio.

AUTHOR NOTE: The first significant publication milestone of my adult writing career, 'Forever 27' (originally entitled 'Vendor') won the 2007 Pearl magazine fiction award. Nothing like validation on this level—the magazine had previously published the likes of Bukowski—to vault my writing career into a higher gear.

PATTERNS OF RECOGNITION

Seth Goodal's had a good time all week on his overdue beach vacation, one that he's needed for so long—relaxation and rest, the order of the day. But only until the last night, and the lunar eclipse. The moon's gravity, affecting more than the tide. Dragging and pulling at his anxiety, quelled and in hiding. For now.

Seth suggests to his wife before nightfall that, for old times' sake, they do a couple of what he calls screamers. Party like back when they were in college, he argues; live it up one last time before returning to the prosaic, workaday world. His wife Alise, noting the fact that not only hadn't they known one another in college, she neither experimented with mind alteration then, nor has any intention of starting at this late date.

Her refusal, posed as query: "Are you kidding?"

So, Seth, alone on the beach, mesmerized and tripping out all on his own. Sickened. Panicked. The umbral moon, swollen and shaded brick as though inflamed with disease, hanging over the indistinct line of the nighttime oceanic horizon. Mottled. Mocking.

Keeping all the pain and fear to himself.

And now the next morning in the car he's got a hangover

head on him, wishing he'd embraced Alise's reticence to imbibe. Seth, guzzling fluids and ruing the screamers, a drive through purgatory if not Hades itself: roadways packed.

The other motorists anger and unnerve Seth. Hurtling wheeled boxes of metal and plastic, fuel tanks strapped onto undercarriages like hidden suicide bombs. Sentient, tender sacks of wet meat trapped inside, belted, restrained. The illusion of safety. He wonders: *How fast is fast enough? Is there an event horizon on the highways of America for* fast-enough, *beyond which one passes back into the realm of sanity?*

Seth's cut off by a trucker. In a rage, he speeds up and at first opportunity, waving a finger and a fist, passes the semi.

Next, a set-piece straight out of *Duel*: the aggressive truck driver hauling a couple of tons of freight chases them down I-95 for twenty miles, tailgating, the driver producing his own hand gesticulations—a dragon, Seth thinks, chasing the cowardly knight, one afraid to stand and fight.

Alise says in a calm soothing reasoned voice, "Chill the eff out, babe. Let the trucks go on their way. After being on vacation, you ought to be more relaxed."

Seth, anything but at ease. Keeping this fact to himself. "Sorry about that. Ready to get home."

"You're driving like someone else."

"Don't be silly—I'm me."

At last he drops out of warp drive, slipping into sub-light speeds and exurban orbit—home, in an outer spiral arm of the city. As automatic as can be, his hand hits the turn signal and he leaves the Eisenhower Interstate Highway System. Can't be right, though; he lives on the other side of town, and yet the subdivision to which he heads, convenient, a mere half-mile off the freeway, is the right destination. Has to be.

And while on the subject of incongruities, his wife's name isn't Alise, it's Elaine.

Yet *Alise* feels right, as does the exit. Were he taking the wrong turn, Alise would speak up, but she makes no protest, continues watching the commercial corridor stream by outside the tinted auto glass, yawns and stretches in anticipation of trip's end.

He has to admit that the screamer sex was fantastic, *la petit mort* like he hasn't felt in many a moon—the screamers, giving one a deep and abiding sense of affection, almost like MDMA. He's heard that hip West Coast headshrinkers sometimes use X in marriage counseling: A rush of empathy to reopen closed pathways, or else salving wounds fresh or otherwise, a treatment working only until the serotonin crash, and the inevitable remembrance of all that's wrong apart from issues of sexual intimacy. Seth is familiar with such matters because lifepartner Alise had been a psychology major, one who now teaches the subject.

The only problem is that Elaine's a philosophy major, one who'd written her thesis on the correspondence theory of truth, with such epistemological matters being the stuff about which he and his wife often speak. A far cry from pharmacological schemes of mental health therapy, yes?

Which wife, though? Confusion.

"I'm having a totally weird déjà vu experience here. Reverse déjà vu. Inverse déjà vu . . ."

"Excuse me?"

". . .transverse déjà vu. Something along those lines."

Widening her eyes, voice low and menacing. "Say 'déjà vu' again. I dare you. I double dare you. Say 'déjà vu' one more goddamn time, motherfucker." Then her hard expression breaks, and she's laughing—earlier in the week they watched *Pulp Fiction* on cable, and for the rest of the vacation she's often lapsed into a menacing 'Jules' persona.

A chuckle. "I'll have a Royale with Cheese, extra mayo on the fries, hold the déjà vu."

"Vincent, that is some repugnant shit." Alise brandishes a thumb-and-forefinger handgun, squeezing the trigger. "*Kablooey.*"

Seth, signaling for the left turn into their neighborhood. "C'mon, I'm serious—I really don't feel like myself."

"How so?"

"Like everything that should feel familiar somehow doesn't? And yet it does."

"Interesting." Elaine stretches again, cracks her neck. No—Alise does, with her long, tanned arms. A beanpole. Elaine was—is—short, cherubic, an angel.

Alise, scrolling through a thousand messages on the Blackberry that she's ignored while away from work—spring break, for the kids, for the professors. "I worried about you partying like that last night—I'm not sure that's a good thing for you to be doing."

"I can't disagree," an echo of screamer tickling at his ganglia. "How about that moon, though? Eerie."

"The moon? What about it?"

"The eclipse. The red moon."

"*Excuse me?*"

A sensation beyond unease settles over him. "Never mind—I must've dreamt it."

"Now that vacation's over, I want you back on the straight and narrow." Stern, then softening her tone. "Okay, honey?"

"Of course."

"I'll unpack and get everything squared away. You can take a nap."

Seth envies Alise: while he's endured having his doors blown off by frenzied fellow drivers, she's dozed away her own hangover —in her case, red wine the culprit instead of a red moon.

Turn, turn, turn, into their quiet, safe neighborhood—and then pulling into the curved driveway of the house. The Goodals. *Welcome.*

Seth's nagging sensation returns—this isn't the right house. Can't be.

The structure's familiar enough—it's a 1970s contemporary, but it's a house he remembers as being one they only *considered* buying, a property that'd had far too many maintenance issues: a cracked foundation, a rotting deck, twin HVAC units in a state of decay, a roof graying with age, sagging gutters overflowing with leaves from the tall hardwoods dotting the sloping, half-acre lot.

This house is the same, yet altered—painted, a newer roof, a rebuilt deck overlooking the woods down the hill. Home. Yet not.

Seth, shaking inside: He remembers standing in this driveway with Elaine looking at the property, but instead settling on the more traditional split-level in the older neighborhood across town, the one closer to her job at the Department of Social Services. The house that seemed more family friendly.

Elaine.

Not Alise.

But then looking over at Alise shoving road-trash into a plastic grocery sack—cellophane from crackers, a diet soda can, a foil packet of pretzels at which she wrinkles her nose. "These were stale. I want my .79 cents back."

Unbuckling his seatbelt. "Hey—look at me."

"What?"

"Nothing." Her features ripple like the heat waves on the highway. Alise. Elaine. Alise. The psychologist.

But Elaine, she loved kids, went into social work because no one goes into the philosophy field except to teach; Elaine, a sensitive type with self confidence issues, thinking she'd never have the stamina to withstand the rigors of the dissertation process. So, switching majors and getting a master's in social work, wanting to help children from abused families—an emotionally bruising, ill-compensated career track. Seth, loving her for this quality. The two of them loving their own child, knowing themselves more than capable of parenting, the polar opposite of Elaine's abuse and neglect cases.

A child.

A daughter. With Elaine, the social worker.

Evelyn.

Elaine. Evelyn. A double E waterfall, cascading over his back.

But at his side, Alise. The two of them, childless by choice.

The facts: Alise, a teacher of psychology at the community college, loves her job, enjoys her students. Proud to help them prepare to either transfer to a more prestigious bastion of higher learning, one such as Southeastern University, or simply for life itself.

Southeastern—a research institute of the first order, the state school, old campus, sprawling, eating up downtown. The institution to which both Elaine and Seth had matriculated.

Except that this isn't Elaine, and the college in question isn't venerable Southeastern University, with its national championship basketball squad and the 'Fighting Redtails' avian mascot and the old antebellum campus that somehow escaped Sherman's marauding arsonists. No, not forty-thousand student Southeastern; instead, he'd met Elaine at Carolina State, a smaller school, a newer institution of modernist architecture in another town a hundred miles away, the mascot a roaring indefatigable Cougar, an ill-respected football team, a more intimate place of higher learning.

Seth, knowing not of Elaine's whereabouts. Further troubling: Who's been minding Evelyn?

But if there is only Alise and no Elaine . . . then what of his daughter?

Getting out of the sedan, which when they'd left a week ago had been a minivan. Seth, asking softly, glancing sidelong across the roof of the car at his wife. "I wonder if Evvie missed us."

Alise, gape-mouthed, staring back at him over the roof of the grayish green vehicle, which ought to be what the dealership called anthracite blue. Alise. "*What did you say?*"

"Evelyn." As his daughter's name escapes his lips, he goes weak in the knees, braces himself against the frame of the car. "I can't remember who's been keeping her."

Concern, confusion. "For heaven's sake. What on earth's wrong with you?"

"This is what I mean—I don't feel right."

"Have you been drinking today?"

Indignant. "*No.*"

Now Seth's wife, whatever her true name, sounds downright fearful. "Jesus—I knew I should've driven."

A moment of clarity: "We don't have a daughter."

Her voice now gentle, cautious. "No, Graham. No, we don't."

"*Graham?*" Temples throbbing, hands itching to consult the identification card within his leather trifold wallet, one that should instead be made out of dyed hemp: Elaine, a vegetarian forbidding the usage of animal skins. "Who the hell's Graham?"

"Are you trying to make some incredibly bad joke?"

Seth, short of breath, his words a thin wheeze. "Sure, honeybunny. You know me and my bad jokes."

"I can't—" Breaking off, searching his eyes. "I can't imagine a worse one."

"World's worst comedian," he says. They begin to pull suitcases from the trunk, which should be the back door of the van.

"That's the thing—I've never known you to be much of a joker."

"Maybe I'm changing."

"I suggest you change back."

Graham—who should be Seth, and still is, as far as he can tell—wonders, still, about his missing daughter, but allows the subject to drop. "By the way—I had a really fun time. I told you we needed that vacation."

"Did you, now? I thought it was my idea."

"Either way, it worked out."

"I wonder. I really do."

Now he's more puzzled than afraid, remembers having had the time of their lives. "What's that supposed to mean?"

"That I'm not sure we solved any of our problems. Not that I expected to, not in ten days."

The trip that Seth took—or the mysterious Graham, as the case may be—only lasted a week, but he allows this discrepancy to go unremarked. "What problems?"

Alise sighs. "I suggested this vacation because, in spite of it all, our marriage means something to me. But—"

"But what?" *And why aren't you calling me Seth, Elaine? Why?*

"I don't think I can go on like this. Not until you're truly better. And I'm starting to worry . . . you won't be. Ever."

Graham's (*Seth's*) mind races. He shakes and feels ill—but not like a hangover. Despite not having stuttered in years, not since prepubescence, he stammers out the next words. "*Guh*-go on like what? Go on like *huh-huh*-how?"

Alise puts a suitcase down on the driveway, yellowed grass growing in the cracks of the weathered and stained concrete. "Let's not do this out here. Please."

"Do what?"

"Start yelling at one another again."

Seth (*Graham*) is dumbfounded. Seth and Elaine (*Alise*) have the strongest marriage of any of their friends—no grave disagreements, no infidelities, comparable interests, compatible bodies and temperaments. And in the form of Evelyn (*Evelyn*), a true life connection.

Evelyn. Who doesn't exist.

"I feel like somebody else."

"I've begged you to get back into therapy. You aren't over it, my dear. Twenty years or not, you are yet to be healed. You need to admit this to yourself."

"Over *what?*"

She offers in reply a stony, suggestive countenance: *This is the kind of shit I'm talking about.*

They unlock the house and go in. The previous owners had cats, a whole brood of them, and after being away long enough the nostrils can still detect a hint of cat urine, a sour, phantom odor. Seth puts the suitcases down in the foyer, walks into the kitchen and runs himself a glass of tap water. He has to open four cabinets to find a drinking glass. Graham would know where the glasses are, but Seth does not.

He decides to ask one more time about Evelyn. "Elaine, honey—?"

From the master suite across the short hallway that leads down into the expansive family room, with its top of the line home theatre and L-shaped sofa, Alise cries out. Seth doesn't care much for movies, neither does Elaine. And yet Graham and Alise do.

She stomps into the kitchen, her face scarlet. "What the hell did you just call me?"

His own cheeks burn. "*Uh-uh*-Alise."

"No, you didn't. Graham, you called me by *her* name," voice breaking. "Again."

"Called you by whose name?"

Alise screams in frustration, picks up a small spiral notebook from the granite countertops (*which should be tile*) and flings it across the cooktop island, pages fluttering like bird's wings. The notebook glances off the hanging copper pots (*stainless steel*) and lands at his feet shod in Nikes (*New Balance*).

Weeping. "How long will I have to play second fiddle to a dead woman?"

"I don't know what you're talking about. I'm hungover. The screamers—the damn pills."

"Pills?" Alise turns pale. "What are you on? Tell me."

"*Nuh*-nothing."

"Why are stuttering? You don't stutter."

"I didn't realize I was *duh-duh*-doing it."

Alise throws up her hands and hurries back into the bedroom. She slams the door, her next words muffled. "You said you were over it, finally. And I believed you."

Over what?

Over Elaine. Over Evelyn.

A brief sensation as though leaning back in a chair starting to tip over.

Ah, thinks he, *of course*. Graham knows this. Seth does not. Seth is unwilling to know these facts. To know, he understands deep down, is to *remember*. That they're both gone.

Images once forestalled now come as a flood:

Elaine walking across campus. Elaine buying the pregnancy test. Both terrified; the result, positive. They'd agreed that *of course we're going to keep the baby: We love each other. We will get married. We will have a daughter; we will name her Evelyn,* she said, *after my grandmother.*

We will buy a house—a cool, contemporary one like the one they saw in the real estate guide, only a half-mile off the beltway, convenient to everything. Impoverished college students, loving one another, talking about matters like how much money they need to buy food in the coming week, what their mutual sets of parents will say when they break the news to them, how the future stands less opaque than ever before in either of their youthful lives, terrifying yet also comforting.

How they look into one another's eyes. How their nighttime wedding is conducted beside a sea splashed by moonlight silvery and pure. How by then she's already starting to show, but no one seems to care and if they do, none say so. How they look at the contemporary house but finally settle on the more traditional one, a down payment the mutual wedding gift from both sets of happy parents.

How they finish their degrees. How Elaine works and Graham *(Seth)* stays home until Evelyn is old enough for day care. How Graham *(Seth)*, an English major, works on a novel, one destined to remain incomplete. How life for a number of years is like tupelo honey.

Until the night on the back road, returning from a Harvest time hay ride.

How the racing teenagers came roaring around the curve, across the double yellow line. How, before the impact, Elaine and Evelyn both cried out; an explosion and a period of black punctuated by a *HUH* sound, what he later realizes is Elaine's death rattle. How he awoke to see his daughter's carseat, upside down, and all quiet and still but for the ticking of the shattered engine, a hissing sound like steam, and the moaning of the other driver from across the road in the opposite ditch—*Help us oh god what happened somebody help us.*

The moon hanging in the sky through the shattered windshield. The veil of blood flowing into his eyes. How in the years afterward he'd tried to write about the accident. How he'd never succeeded.

How he sees his dead daughter in the faces of the town's high school students, which is how old Evelyn would be by now. Thinking how much she and her mother resemble one another, and would continue to do so into Evvie's adulthood.

How in the years since the accident he's pursued a random and purposeless serious of occupations, none of which make him happy, none of which can replace the ache inside him over tragedies now long ago. How he's dying inside bit by bit, and has been for years, hiding this from Alise, from the world.

How he's functional. And happy.

Yet not.

Seth pours himself another glass of water but forgets to switch on the filter. How the water tastes of chlorine; how he'd expected sweet and clean.

He goes down the spiral staircase to the family room. The house seems much too big for the two of them, a hollow cavern. Trying for a child here and there, Seth (*Graham*) hoping in secret not to succeed, his wish coming true. Talk of a seeing a fertility specialist, but talk like that withering on the vine. Graham (*Seth*) in no shape to be a father. Not anymore.

Hearing Alise standing above him on the loft, the high ground. "Don't people get over things? Eventually?"

Quiet, to himself. "You were the psych major."

He eases onto the couch and makes a sound like AHHHH, the way exhausted people do when they finally get to sit down. The sofa feels much more firm that he expected—he'd hoped to sink into the cushions, perhaps swallowed up by the sofa like the bed eating the kid in that old horror movie. The one to which he'd taken Elaine on their first date, when they had been but teenagers swept up in a clammy-palmed rush of hormonal intoxication. A movie about nightmares.

Is he Graham, or Seth? He doesn't feel like Graham at all. Seth feels like an altogether different person from Graham.

Graham died that night too. Or perhaps Seth. Or perhaps both.

Seth.

Graham remembers with a sick stab of fresh grief: *Seth.*

Seth was what they had chosen to name their second child, as yet unborn. How the ultrasound had shown a healthy baby—a boy. Only a week before the Harvest Hayride.

Graham, all but unhurt, walking away from the wrecked minivan, but she—they—unable to do so.

Or only a dream, a bad dream? No—a scar on his forehead the reminder of their smiles, the long-healed remnant of a wound from which blood had flowed into his eyes and colored the moon red.

He fingers his hairline, finds the bumpy escarpment of tissue: The scar is there; the scar is real.

Graham picks up the universal remote—a learning device, a single gadget to control the different electronic machines in the entertainment system. He doesn't remember buying any of the gear, has to squint at the buttons to see which one turns on the power to the TV set. He can see his reflection in the gray of the widescreen: indeed, it is Graham sitting on the couch. Lumpen, inert, but himself. Indisputable.

Perhaps all this is the happy dream of a regular, good life. Perhaps Graham perished in the accident alongside them, and all this but a dream flashing by at the instant of his death.

Graham gets up and goes to the window, rests his elbow on the edge of the television monitor, checks to make sure it is solid and not a dream. He squints out at the burgeoning greenery of springtime, and the slope leading down to a gurgling brook that's cut through the land for eons, forcing a *V* in the small patch of woods separating the houses from the other side of the neighborhood. The stream rushes through its channel, spots of foam at several points where diminutive waterfalls gurgle.

He goes out on the deck and down the stairs to the yard below, shuffling toward the stream through leaves and underbrush that need raking. He intends to lie down in the water, hoping for the creek to carry him to the river flowing to the East, one that joins with another river and then another still before fanning into a great delta meeting the roiling green sea from which the Goodals have only now returned. The ocean, its tides tugged and cajoled by a moon of pearl, the waters vast enough to swallow him whole: A different sort of vacation.

But Graham's is a ridiculous, ruinous desire. The creek—unlike the memories he has sought to obliterate—isn't able to transport a fully grown man to a different place. Only the man himself holds such power.

Graham rolls up his khakis and takes off his shoes and gets in the water anyway; standing with its modest current coursing around his ankles, he splashes his face. He breathes deep and holds his arms up to the under-canopy of the trees, and the shimmering sunlight beyond. He feels Seth leave him, feels Elaine and Evelyn go back to sleep again. By force of will, he tells them good-bye. Again.

Alise, watching him from the deck. "Now what are you doing?"

Graham, looking at his wife as though seeing her for the first time in a long time—for the first time ever. "I had beach sand between my toes."

Alise, laughing. "It lingers in the cracks, doesn't it?"

"Yes." Graham, washed in the lifeblood of the stream, renewed, reborn, a man neither of past nor future, only the moment at hand: "But it doesn't have to."

AUTHOR NOTE: Published on Fiction365.com in early 2013, this personal favorite story of mine garnered one of the widest readerships of my writing career.

BOYCRAZY

The mother's hands, tremulous, clutched at her daughter's diary, an ordinary schoolhouse notebook. Its lined pages, splayed wide open to the girl's innermost secrets.

Shocking secrets to which no mother should be privy.

Ever.

No decent mother, anyway.

With every sordid revelation, Flora Mae Harkin, a member of the First Baptist Church as well as the Edgewater Ladies Munificence Society, fought to keep her powder dry.

The shame—the shame of it all.

After a few more lurid passages—her daughter, engaging in intercourse with everyone from high school boys to married men —Flora Mae focused less on the bubble-shaped teen girl's handwriting than the arthritic knuckles curled around the cover of the book. Her fingers, bony and knobby like her mother's and her grandmother's before that, as though her bloodline born to work as stevedores or field hands instead of housewives.

Despite the shock of the revelations, one specific aside left her apoplectic:

My worst problem, when you get right down to brass tacks as they say, is that my mother does not understand me.

My mother doesn't understand me.

My mother doesn't understand me!

There, I wrote it, and dang if I don't mean it.

I am not even sure she isn't losing her dang mind. Since Daddy died, she's been like there is a wall around her. But then she's always been that way, hasn't she? Of course she has. Not even Daddy dying could change that old henhouse biddy.

Emma Jane's words sliced Flora Mae like the time at Thanksgiving when the cleaver slipped, and she had lost the tip of her little finger. Blood everywhere. A turkey that'd taken the better part of two days to prepare, ruined.

After all the other salacious details—appalling enough in their specificity—the notion of being *lacking in maternal understanding* had been what slapped her out of a foggy fugue state induced by the profane ledger: Flora Mae, no amateur in this game of childrearing, and Emma Jane far from her first, though certainly the last. Short of taking in a waif from a relative due to some unforeseen misadventure, which of course she would do if called upon, Flora Mae Harkin's ability and motivation to care for children felt exhausted.

One never knew, though. What one would do. If called to serve.

Based on how she'd been reared? The decision had better be to serve.

But so tired of it all.

Tired right from the day fifteen years earlier when Doc Boykin had said, "Well, this ain't one for the Guinness Book, but ma'am? I'm right surprised to declare that you're with child."

Told him he must be joking.

"No joke."

"But the change, it's underway. It simply cannot be."

The doctor, winking at her. "All it means is that you and your husband are still in love. That's all."

She'd cussed a blue streak all the way home. Here she'd been looking forward to the day when DeWayne would be old enough to go into the Navy like Horton, but instead? Starting again with another squalling infant on her hip.

No—she hadn't felt angry about Emma Jane. Only fatigued.

Tired all through the unexpected pregnancy. Tired through Emma's toddler years, those terrible twos that seemed to go on and on; the colics and fevers and ear infections the girl finally outgrew. Tired anew as Flora Mae's arthritis grew intolerable. And tired now of the pains in her upper back, some kind of bursitis that radiated down her arm. And the headaches.

Worn to a nub. Thirty years of children running up and down the stairs the way Emma still did, like a herd of mules stampeding across the heart-of-pine floors.

It was understandable to feel put upon: All the rigmarole from Horton's sudden death. The matters of probate and the estate. Selling off a parcel of the old farmland to some fool wanting to build houses on it. Not to mention DeWayne and Nadine, two grown adults, all but clawing at each other's throats over who got left what.

All the children, grown or otherwise, disloyal. Running wild on her.

One task to which Flora Mae didn't cotton would be rearing her own teenage daughter's child. Which if it hadn't happened yet, would soon occur—if the diary entries rang true, the law of averages, already stretched to its limit.

Her daughter, the town strumpet. Now the pair of red high heels discovered during last week's snooping made sense.

Mercy. Not another infant in the house.

Her daughter, brash and sloe-eyed, in the full flower of her burgeoning womanhood. Auburn hair cut Peggy Sue style, with darling little flips. Breasts and hips rounded, fingers and toes painted scarlet. Emma Jane, a beauty. No doubt.

All the more reason to remain chaste. Or at least choosy, for heaven's sake.

Groaning as though in physical pain, Flora Mae snapped shut the diary and slid it back into the dresser drawer. Considered leaving it out so the girl would realize that her perfidies and profligacies had been revealed, revelatory, like the opening of the seventh seal.

~

AFTER LIGHTING A SLENDER, afternoon cigarette—Flora Mae's sole vice—she eased onto the porch swing to wait. The countryside, peaceful until an aircraft zoomed overhead. She remembered how President Eisenhower was to speak on television that night about the Russians, and the bomb. People were building shelters in their backyards, stockpiling canned food. The world could end any day.

The future felt as though it had arrived.

And Emma Jane Harkin's response? Spreading her legs like a common trollop.

As the smoke settled her nerves, Flora Mae made up her mind about the diary. She hurried back upstairs to leave it open on her daughter's bedspread, still crisp and new from the Sears department store down in Columbia.

Spoiled, this child. And ungrateful.

Her mind racing, Flora Mae went to prepare dinner. Chicken. Horton insisted on chicken every Friday night, and despite his absence, she'd maintained the tradition.

Grease. Perhaps that's what had killed him.

P'shaw.

Hearing the front door open and close. Her daughter's footfalls, approaching the kitchen, but stopping. Heading upstairs instead. To her room.

Emma Jane's scream, muffled by the ceiling.

~

A FEW MOMENTS LATER, the girl, clutching a stack of textbooks, appeared in the kitchen doorway. Her voice, quavering. "I'm going to the county library to study. I got a test tomorrow."

"You *have* a test tomorrow."

"S'what I said."

"You said, 'got.' I didn't teach you to talk like a common street urchin."

Chewing her lip. "Like I said. I got to go back out."

Continuing to bread chicken thighs and drumsticks on the counter by the sink, Flora Mae kept her tone steady. "You'll do no such thing. Sit."

"Don't talk to me like I'm a child—*Mother*."

Emma had taken to calling her 'mother' rather than 'mama.' The formality made the honorable title feel like an epithet. "You are most certainly still a child."

"No. I haven't been one for some time, now."

"So I understand."

Emma. Hooded eyes. Holding her gaze. "*How dare you.*"

"Me? I hope your Daddy's paying scant attention to your—your—" The right words, escaping her. "Your lack of discretion."

At last the girl plopped down in a heap. Laid her head on the table. From inside crossed arms: "I can't believe you took and read my diary."

Fury, bubbling over like a forgotten pot of grits left on high heat. "Running with those walleyed, no-good Macon boys? Hanging around Mr. Rabon's Esso station? You're better than that, young lady." An aside, like one of Edward R. Murrow's editorials: "What you need is to study your scriptures, and get your smart-talking posterior inside a church. Many of Edgewater County's less savory denizens would be doubly behooved to do so, if they're to live eternally with us in the Kingdom of Heaven. They should begin their redemption by avoiding that awful Dixiana roadhouse, brazen and sinful there alongside the town common."

Her daughter's face, sour. "Such a hypocrite."

"I'd never set foot in a place like that tavern."

"I'm talking about church."

The truth of it stung—since Horton passed, they had been remiss about attending services. Whenever challenged about their rank truancy by the pastor or the ladies at Ruth's Beauty Shop, Flora Mae insisted she remained 'still too tender' to sit in the sanctuary where her husband's body had so recently lain. Her face flamed hot as the skillet into which she plopped the pieces of breaded chicken, oil splattering and sputtering.

"Lord, I admit that do I need to be in Thy presence more often."

"Bullcorn."

"Prayer. Obedience. *Chastity*." Her throat, swelling with the word. "You must embody these ideals."

"I don't mind going to church." Emma, coy, flashed mascaraed eyelashes. She rested her chin on a fist as though posing for an Olan Mills portrait. "Over at Gethsemane, there's so many nice boys—devout boys."

The girl knew what buttons to push. The thought of those tongue-talkers gesticulating with ostentatious abandon made Flora Mae's skin crawl. The snake handling at Gethsemane Pentecostal Holiness church didn't seem much more wholesome than drinking alcohol at a honkytonk like The Dixiana.

She swept excess flour, corn meal, and spice mix from the counter top into the ceramic sink Horton had planned to replace with stainless steel. "You think after I lie down for the night I haven't noticed you going out that window?"

"I ain't out doing nothing any normal young woman oughtn't do."

"You shame us." Flora Mae couldn't raise her sight. "And don't say 'ain't'."

"Mama—you're just old. That's your problem."

In truth, Flora Mae hadn't noticed the comings and goings. Since Horton passed, she'd begun a program of sleeping tablets that Dr. Boykin prescribed. She hated relying on the medicine, but needed rest.

Dreamless sleep. Would it deign to come.

Nevertheless: "This licentious behavior, it-has-to-stop," tapping in time on the flour-strewn Formica. "Before you get into real trouble."

"I'm being careful. I ain't—I'm not running around."

She bade her daughter to stop with the lies. "You have proper boyfriends you're willing to bring into your father's living room, then?"

"I ain't got a father to bring no one home to. Not a normal home."

"Based on what I've been reading? I don't see anything normal about you."

"Hey, warden, your chicken's smoking—!"

The meat had begun to burn.

Flora stabbed and hacked at the iron skillet with the crooked old spatula she preferred over the newer one. The breasts and thighs had turned black on one side, while still raw on the other. Acrid smoke fouled the air. A catastrophe. As though she'd never fried a dad-blamed chicken in her life.

Her voice, breaking like brittle glass. "The meal—*it's ruined.*"

"It ain't nothing but the same old fried chicken. Big deal."

In awe: "What a reprehensible thing to say to one's own devoted mother."

That shrug of hers. The eye rolling. "Ain't hungry anyway."

The crisis abating, Flora switched on the stovetop fan. A lump had formed in her throat. She rued the mess.

Emma Jane rose and leaned against the wall beneath the fine-carved gingerbread clock that had hung there for the entirety of Flora Mae's life, the dutiful pendulum swinging with silent, graceful regularity. "It's lonely here—you're like a room in the house nobody ever goes in."

Flora, hunched over the counter, ignored her child's nonsense.

Unbidden, the impertinent red-haired princess continued. "And since Daddy? You're worse than ever."

"You're talking foolishness, now." Hot tears stung at the

corners of her eyes. Flora Mae's words came breathy and weak. "Just hush up that smart mouth."

Emma snorted. "It's like you ain't even here half the time. Not for me, anyway."

"I suppose you're angling for some sugar daddy to come along? To take care of you, little miss roundheel?"

"You ain't never acted like you wanted me here. So, sure—why not?"

"P'shaw," all she could muster.

Smarmy and profane: "I'm not the only person around here who could use one."

A pain, radiating in Flora Mae's upper back. "Hush your recalcitrant mouth."

"You know it's true."

Flinging pieces of fouled chicken into the wastebasket. "How can you say these vile things to your own mother?"

"When someone's aching to feel loved, there's no telling what she'll do." Defiant now, Emma Jane, no longer concerned with pretense. "That's why I sneak out to be with boys—and yes, with men. To feel less lonely."

"What would a child know about loneliness?"

The indignity of the diary paled compared to what came next: the assertion that Emma Jane would be going to live in Raleigh with her grown sister. In "a real place," as she put it. "I'm getting out of Edgewater County. Before I get swallowed up."

Nadine, with a girl nearly Emma's age—Sally, a flaxen haired angel, named for her great grandmother. Flora Mae's first grandchild. "You'll do no such thing."

"Nadine says that if I want, I can stay and finish high school there."

"So now y'all are plotting behind my back? My own daughters?"

The girl, snickering as though watching Milton Berle wearing a dress on that coarse television program of his. "It wasn't no plot. I just asked. And she said, sure thing."

Flora Mae sucked wind, fought not to sob. A fly, bashing its tiny head against the glass of a window that needed cleaning. The fan, squeaking as it rotated back and forth and fluttering the pages of that morning's *Edgewater Advocate*, still folded and unread. Horton's paper. Despite her civic duties as a member of the ELMS, she couldn't care less about the business and news of the day in downtown Tillman Falls. Not anymore.

Flora Mae suffered a spell—she flashed on her own teenage years. Being courted by Horton. Squired to the Confederate Jasmine Dance. How he'd shown such interest. Had been so handsome and upstanding, the son of an elder Mason and town father. Standing outside the armory—how he had kissed her with such impertinence. And the crackling electricity of his lips, sending her zooming away into the spring night, in motion without moving at all:

At his touch, she had floated.

She'd become crazy for Horton Harkin of Edgewater County. Thought about him day and night. A catch. Flora Mae grabbed hold, had never let loose. Her first and only.

Her late husband.

Flora Mae felt more than heard the heavy front door slam, hard enough to rattle the silverware in the dish rack. She hadn't noticed that Emma Jane had left the kitchen.

"Just go on to Raleigh." Flora Mae, nonchalant. "We'll see how long that lasts."

But in the fullness of her solitude, Flora Mae collapsed onto the chair where her daughter had sat. Wailed like a common negro at one of their drawn out funerals. Flung Horton's newspaper onto the checkerboard pattern of the tile floor.

Had she cried like this for him? For her own husband?

No. At the service, not a single tear. Dignified, staid, steadfast. The children, they had done all the crying. And the townspeople, including the women at the beauty shop, they had stood in quiet, studied admiration of her constancy.

Strength. For her children. Her family.

The survivors.

EXHAUSTED by the strife and worry, later that night she waited in the formal living room for her daughter to return home, but fell into a fitful asleep. Massive, the weight on her soul. Literal—a heaviness in the center of her chest.

In dreams, she chased after cherubic Emma Jane. A toddler, running and laughing, farther and farther away down the yellow dirt road upon which Flora Mae had once walked to the schoolhouse. Again and again, the child, merry and insouciant, ran ahead. Unreachable.

Far from frightening Flora, this looping, purgatorial interlude made her body feel light as gossamer. Finally she seemed to drift high above the verdant, rolling Edgewater County farmland. Weightless, like dandelion fluff.

Within the dream she became aware of herself, and the fact that she was dreaming—the oddest sensation! The thought came: If only she could maintain this feeling, why, she wouldn't need anyone at all. Once she finally awoke, Flora Mae Harkin could simply float.

AUTHOR NOTE: A prequel of a sort to the collection's title story, the previously unpublished 'Boycrazy' not only presages the events that will 'cancel Christmas,' but fits into the overall Edgewater County mythology at the heart of my fiction.

TRUE GOSPEL

In September a hurricane is forecast to roll through South Carolina like it owns the place. Despite our city being a hundred miles inland, the big blow is still expected to lay down wicked damage. Power out. Trees down. A real mess, as the talking heads predict.

Best part? Classes at our downtown university—a major one —get canceled.

Which means: Time to prepare; big opportunity to party.

To this end, on the evening of Hugo's landfall my friend and I decide to hang out at his duplex in the Arcadia Mills neighborhood near campus. Drink a few beers. Toke up on some kind bud we scored, sticky nugs that stink to high heaven. Do some acid. Semester's been underway for a month, but we're still in summertime mode. Should last until about Thanksgiving.

We sit on his front porch and watch the sky darkening.

"You feeling anything yet?"

"Give it time." We got it at the Dead shows in August, perforated sheets of blue pasteboard imprinted with tiny silver lightning bolts. Heady stuff. "Patience, grasshopper."

"Maybe it went bad, Tim-bo."

"It's been in the freezer." I can feel the waves already coming on, not unlike the rising surf already pounding the low country shoreline. "Let it happen."

"Maybe we should do another one."

That's Freddie for you—always like, let's-do-some-more. "Dude."

"My resistance is high."

He's got a point. We drop another one. Gonna be a long night.

An eerie stillness settles outside the old mill house here in a crime-ridden neighborhood populated by college kids alongside poor folks and crackheads and retiree oldtimers who used to work at the mill, which finally shut down last year. I hope that Freddie's pad, over sixty years old and made of wood, with its last paint job peeling off the siding in long strips that dangle in the gusting, desultory pre-storm breeze, won't get blown to matchsticks.

Crazy quiet. My stomach's tight. I drink a beer, which only makes me feel more bloated. Maybe I should've stayed in my dorm room, a building that's solid, made of concrete. But Freddie has a way of talking me into stuff.

The wind picks up.

And the rains begin.

We head inside to get stoned.

AT THREE IN the morning the storm's peak matches that of our raging acid high, and we traipse outside into the street. All the neighbors are wisely buttoned up inside their houses.

Tripping balls, we laugh and howl with the wind.

Enormous trees whip back and forth; snapping sounds come to us from deep in the unseen unknown beyond the gray wall. Shingles fly off the steep, pitched roofs of the houses, a design called a saltbox. Trash blows around from a couple of overturned herbie-curbies. Rain falls sideways, soaks our T-shirts and shorts. We don't care.

Freddie, pupils dilated, hair blowing back from his round face: "*Feel that power?*"

My temples throb—with or without the hurricane, all would be swirling. Good acid, straight from the motherland. "It's immense."

"It's *what?*"

"It's big, dude."

All Freddie can do over the roar of the storm is yell *IT'S WHAT?* again.

Unable to convey the sense of immensity I feel, I flap my arms.

Freddie starts flapping his arms, too. "How high can we try! How high can we try!" A mantra.

With an eerie suddenness, however, the eye wall of the storm arrives, and all at once the wind and rain peter out. Sprinkles and drizzles, now, but the roar of harsher weather remains in the distance like the trains that rumble through the neighborhood at all hours.

"Whoa."

Freddie, awed. "Like the guy on the TV predicted . . . double whoa."

"Now that feels like power. Dude foresaw this happening, bro."

The words roll like marbles off a tongue that feels thickened. I can see glowing golden streaks like dancing angels, but after contemplating the likelihood, I realize it's only candles flickering in the windows of the houses—the juice, the precious juice, has gone out.

Freddie, grabbing at the back of his neck. "It's like, profound. And all."

My lips crackle. I convince myself that I'm thirsty. "Totally."

The wind picks up. Lightning flashes. Shit's getting real again.

Freddie, contemplative. "We got enough beer?"

"I don't even feel the beer anymore."

"True enough."

We go back inside to watch the walls melt and smoke more of the weed, which won't do much for us either. With classes canceled, it's a long weekend. Sweet.

Wait—did I mention that already, about canceled classes?

❧

THAT NEXT WEEK the Southeast cleans itself up, and for most of us life returns to normalcy.

Almost from the moment Freddie suggests a particular idea, however, I get a weird vibration that must be connected with all the unsettled energy left in the storm's wake. My grandfather, Grandy Latham, once told me that intuition is already there inside everyone, but you've also got to develop it to fully get in its groove. Third eye stuff. He'd never have called it that. But wise, my granddad.

Freddie's point about how much money we'll make by driving down to Sedge Island, though, it's like, totally undeniable: For the trouble of this modest jaunt to the coast, we'll come home with as much as a grand—big profit, in other words, and all in exchange for the extra sheets of acid I brought back from Dead tour.

Harmless enough of a so-called criminal trade. Just slinging a bit of cheap, wholesale tour doses for extra spending money back home.

And having paper on hand, that's really helped with Grandy's third-eye development routine. I've been dosing first thing in the morning, going to class, getting on with the day. It's rad. My grades are sharp as they ever were, at least in spirit, and it's not even midterms yet.

My dad hates all this Deadhead crap, as would my grandfather, if he were alive to see how long my hair's gotten. How I've grown out a beard and wear Birkenstocks. Dad warns for me to keep up with my studies, which I do. Says he's paying for school, so I better bring home the grades. And get a freaking haircut, which I'm not doing.

He's always so worried about what I'm spending money on. Mama doesn't seem to care, bless her heart, but I know she hates my hobbies, too.

Sorry, y'all. The music, and the scene, it moves me.

But a cash-headstash? Yeah. Maybe Freddie's right. It would be sick to have bucks to do a few shows on the fall tour, but also, like, fly out for New Year's in San Francisco? It's 1989, and a new dickhead—I mean, decade—is coming.

Plus: I can always bring back more doses to cover expenses for the spring semester. Sling them around campus. Safe as kittens.

I wish I could explain my capitalistic endeavors to my father. I know he'd be proud of my ambition, but dude manages a grocery store back home in my small Southern town. Goes to church. He's a barrel-chested country boy who keeps his hair short as tennis ball fuzz. Works on cars, listens to old-timey country music and stands up at the high school football games, hand over heart, when the marching band my sister's in plays the national anthem. My mother was his only girlfriend. He gets his worldview from CBS News. All he knows about the Dead is from that Harry Reasoner piece about the Haight back in 1967. Thinks nothing of the band's music or sociological impact, only that they were spitting on servicemen coming back home from overseas. Which is bunk. The Dead stay out of politics.

"If you get into trouble running with this bunch," he had threatened, "and I mean trouble on another level besides them turd-hunt grades last term?"

"Yes, sir?

"You're gonna be on your own."

"Grades'll be better. Hang tight."

"Hang what, now?"

"Relax."

He had scoffed at me. "Just keep your head on your shoulders and your skinny butt buried in them expensive-ass books of your'n. Don't ever forget, you're the first Latham to go to college."

Heavy. I assured him, and continue to do so, that I will. That I can go to music concerts, yet not waste money. And still hit the books, too.

College has changed me. Made me understand the requirements of adulthood, the main one being to keep a headstash together. In the spring I've decided to move into the Mass Comm advertising track instead of majoring in English. Money to be made in that trade, and it's creative.

But still, my dad wonders how I can afford to do all the concerts. How the T-shirts I claim to sell to people in the parking lot, a mild fib, must be real nice and all.

My folks, they'd crap if they knew what I do to make money. Hope they never find out.

IN THIS VEIN, it seems Freddie's buddy, a beach bum-slash-bartender from the coast, is looking to score paper—quantity, like a couple of sheets, a few hundred doses, nothing major, whatever he can get his hands on. The story is that it's dry as hell down there, or so Freddie's friend Hayne whined over the phone.

It really would be worth my while. I scored the 'cid from some kind Bay Area bus people for fifty cents a hit and sell it around campus in ten-strips for thirty or forty bucks, depending, but this guy says he'll lay down five hundred a sheet.

A ten-time markup.

Sweet.

But it's not only fat profit for me. Freddie says that down there? Hayne'll go on to sell doses to vacationers and barflies and random partiers and other beach bums, as Hayne tells Freddie, for like, ten bucks a hit. "Without breaking a sweat."

"Fat wallets down there. Vacation."

"Ain't America great?"

Sedge Island's a swanky destination. It's the kinda resort town in which people like a famous movie producer and a weirdo rock star live in an exclusive enclave full of mansions that cost in the millions.

Who the hell are they, these rich people?

Where does money come from?

I'll tell you: From human endeavor. Business. A trade.

On my micro-level, what's to mull over? My buddy's buddy needs paper, and in a magical, cosmic confluence of synchronicity, I happen to have paper. As established, I'd always thought of the island as being more of a coke town, but whatever.

At the dining hall, eating burritos and nachos off plastic trays molded in Southeastern Redtails burgundy, I get a flash of this-doesn't-feel-right.

"You sure about this deal?"

Shredded lettuce hangs off his scraggy beard, which grows in all patchy—he's one of those dudes who can't muster a full one. "A chunk of change, one fell swoop? No brainer. None of this parceling out doses to dumb frat boys like we been doing. Work smart, not hard."

"Trust the guy?"

Blowing out his lips, Fredo says Hayne Williamson is an old friend from school days. Like, childhood and shit. "All the way back to second grade."

"Long as you're sure."

"Hayne, he's good people."

"He better be."

"Have faith, bro."

FREDDIE, you have to love the guy. Biggest stoner I know; always the best bud. Good man to have onboard the starship. He's a real character, a lumbering, ginger-colored life-sized hippy Muppet, full lips and bugging eyes with heavy dark eyelids that blink like they're hinged, and ought to have their own sound effect—*plink! plink!*—like a high C on a piano. He's got a kinky, red afro he keeps pulled back into a big honking ponytail, and a set of crusty, oversized feet with rounded cartoon toes peeking over the edges of filthy Birks missing cork at both ends. When he's high? Like, really high? Gets a look on his face like the Buddha. Placid like a lake in summertime.

But yeah, Muppet feet—get your mind around it. That's one part of a Muppet you don't normally see.

Except for Big Bird.

And Fozzie Bear.

And Mr. Snuffleupagus.

Never mind.

"I don't know why you're being so squirrelly about Hayne." Freddie's redneck-hippie patois tumbles without urgency through a cloud of blue smoke from a bomber he's torquing up off one of those long fireplace lighters. Bogarts with another big hit.

"Just trying to be careful." I put on a stentorian, Joe Friday cop voice. "This LSD, it's a serious, dangerous drug. People who deal it should be behind bars."

We both laugh and high five. Smoking and exhaling, mugging like a breakout sidekick character on a sitcom, Freddie says, "Hayne loves me—*who don't, though*?"

"He's all right? He's down?"

"Down as up is."

I grapple with the concept. "Do what, now?"

"He's down. He's a kind brother."

"Man, you better be sure." In my own voice this time: "Serious business, this drug dealing. Serious crime."

"On the way down we'll get to eyeball cool storm damage. A billion freaking dollars' worth, bro."

"That's a lotta doses."

"Damn—that would be awesome. We could get everybody in the world high with that much acid."

Fredo and I snort with mirth and bump fists. He twists up a fresh fatty from a dirty frisbee of weed and rolling papers on his lap. We get stoned. It's chill.

~

BUT MY ANTENNAE KEEP TWITCHING, like an itch you can't reach.

Been getting more cautious and paranoid anyways: back during the spring semester some heads we kinda halfway know got stung holding big-time, a dude and his old lady we hung with at the Charlotte shows a year ago. And it wasn't just like city cops— the DEA rolled in on those kids too. Story goes they had a party, some dude came they didn't know, and somebody sold dude a ten-strip. Next day? The kids get raided, right in the middle of pulling tubes and eating Rice Krispies.

Feds.

Ouch.

Freddie and our friend Neill and me, sitting around getting baked one afternoon, got the dope on the bust from this chick Sally who had swung by after class to drop off nugs. We sat nodding and shaking our heads, knowing those poor cats were only tour kids holding sheets they'd brought home to share with friends. Not dealers. Reading about them in the paper made me feel like you do when you're on tour and see some kind brothers and sisters being searched along the roadside. When you see that the cops have a K-9 unit. When you see kids, tie-dyed and inno-cent, leaning against the sunstruck windows of their VW bus. Heads hanging. Fucked.

Found among the possessions of the alleged LSD dealers, read the newspaper story, *were tickets for the upcoming Grateful Dead European tour*. From this fact the police chief got all deductive, boasting in the media that this time he'd snagged some big squirming fish on his lawman's cane pole. Characterized the bust as part of an apparent "international drug ring." Cue ominous organ swell.

Drug-ring my eye. Just kids slinging a little paper.

Getting a headstash together.

For the next tour.

Like me.

Huh.

~

EPIGRAPH for the rest of the week, courtesy the Talking Heads: *The island of doubt, it's like the taste of medicine.*

In other words? I can't shake the paranoia.

While we trudge up the hill to the Union to get sub sandwiches for dinner and maybe shoot a game of pool, I again bring up the doses-deal with Hayne. How my pineal gland quivers about it. I chant a mantra at Freddie: I dunno, I dunno, I dunno.

Wearied by my niggling worries. "Dude, believe me—I am more than sure about m'boy Hayne. We were in freaking Boy Scouts." Conspiratorial. "We had a freaking circle jerk together in the woods, bro."

"He better be family. S'all I'm saying."

"Hayne's my boy, dude."

I belch oil and vinegar and rack up a game of nine-ball on the pitted and stained green felt, remembering how I once turned a cup of coffee over on this very table, one morning when I was cutting a history class that'd been boring me to tears.

As I stand off to the side waiting for Freddie to break, I'm overcome by the urge to take one last stab at bailing:

"Dude."

"What?"

"Let me just front it."

"Hayne's got money. He don't need it on the front."

"What I mean is: Take him whatever he needs. This weekend's like, inconvenient. I got shit to do."

"'Shit to do?'" *Plink-plink* go the eyelids.

"I got homework piling up—and laundry, et cetera."

Fredo, aghast: "Homework? *Laundry?*"

Shrugging. "It bites."

"It can wait."

"And if it can't?"

"Lemme paint a picture for you: We'll stay on the island all weekend. Get in some beach time. Troll for betties. Get loose. Get laid."

"I must say you have an excellent point there," sounding like the Russian ambassador in *Dr. Strangelove.* In my own voice: "Been awhile since I got laid."

"Gonna be sweet."

Freddie's break is explosive, but no balls fall and he calls bullshit on his shitty, warped house cue. I shoot at the one ball, a slight miscue that makes me feel like a newbie.

"Thing is, I'm really behind in a couple of classes."

"Who ain't?" He drops the one, followed by the two on a banking shot that indeed makes me look like an amateur. Walks the cue ball down the rail and drops the three. Spins the stick and dances around like Tom Cruise showing off for Paul Newman before dropping the purple four in the side on a simple bank shot. "C'mon, Timmy. I'll even let you win—I'll scratch on the nine."

Not only am I beaten down by his cajoling, I have to stand and watch the asshole run the table on me including the nine, which costs me five bucks along with a fresh agreement to hit the island and meet up with Hayne.

But still, I hate the thought of driving again with all those doses. Considering that I made it all the way home without so much as a wink or a nod from the heat—on a plane, no less— makes travel seem like asking for trouble.

THE MORE I think about it, though, I feel for the guy—Fredo's buddy. We park our cars in the same garage. A friend in need, and so on. We had a weed drought here last summer for about a month. Super lame.

I'm sure it *is* real dry down there, and not simply for the more exotic psychedelics like these clean West Coast doses: a few weeks back I read in the paper about another big bust, this one a Major Narcotics Operation on Sedge Island, as the headline screamed.

The narcs nabbed some cat with a regular black market pharmacopoeia at hand, locked and loaded and stocked up like the Walgreen's: Doses, shrooms, and weed. The tour staples, yeah yeah, not the white powders. But this dude must not have been a hippy kid, because he was also slinging speed, blow, crank, X, Valium, Vicodin, Special K, two different kinds of regulated anabolic steroids, and fucking horse tranquilizers. So, being that it sounds like they tagged a main guy, no wonder Hayne's looking off-island to score. Whomever else deals on the island would be laying low. Take away the tourists, as Freddie has described it, and what you have left is a small town.

In a tourist Mecca like Sedge Island, somebody'll come along soon to fill the void. They always do. The black market's like any other capitalist market—if there's a need, someone'll sniff out the opportunity and fill it. ECON taught me this.

Toking up in my room before afternoon classes—two hits and the joint's turned brown—I keep on whining.

"I do need to get some shit done. S'all I'm saying." Grabbing my book bag covered in rock-logo patches, I make to leave. "Do laundry, et cetera."

Did I say that already? Or just think it?

Fredo, snagging the bone and tucking it into the corner of his mouth for a nice long toke. "You with the laundry again. Gotta get your priorities straight."

I crumble in the face of this logic. "Okay. Tell Hayne we'll jet down there."

Puff, puff. Hands it back. Smoke from his nostrils in two mighty plumes. "I already did."

I hand back the smoldering, resinous bomber and go to wash my hands before class. Who the hell smokes joints anymore? Fredo, that's who, because he dropped and broke his prized glass bowl.

~

So now it's after lunch on Friday. I'm again blowing off the self-paced Astronomy units. It's more sub sandwiches. It's gassing up the car. It's that feeling you get when you're about to head out of town for a few days to the beach, a sense of adventure. My family went to Surfside in the summer. Sedge Island, again, that's a rich person's place.

For half a sec we debate the idea of throwing some beer in the cooler to sip on over the course of the drive; think better of it.

Sober as judges—calm, collected, eyes clear and bright—we hit the bricks with a head of steam. Secret agents on a mission of mercy. Pop in a tape, a second set from last summer. Debate hitting the Sneak-a-Toke™ I've packed full of kind bud. Decide *nah*.

"Not till we get onto the island. Then we can puff and chill."

"Right on."

After we negotiate the big interstate interchange halfway to Charleston, we're southbound on 95 looking fine as wine. But now we find ourselves on the most dangerous stretch of the journey, the good old mainline drug conduit of the eastern seaboard.

But we've taken precautions. Both our cars back home, see, are covered in colorful Dead stickers, so instead we borrowed Fredo's brother's ride, a Lincoln Continental with no dancing bears or peace signs or other ill-advised signifiers. In fact, it's a former unmarked cop car he bought at an auction yard for like, a thousand bucks. In this boat, like some grandfather's car, we probably look like cops ourselves.

Furthermore, I've got my hair stuffed under a burgundy Redtails ball cap. Fredo's made precious little concession to disguising his wiry bundle of near-dreadlocks, though, the volume of which is gathered back by a fading hemp hair-tie that stinks to high heaven. Clothing: Polo shirts, khaki shorts. Nikes instead of tie-dyes and Birks. Other than the hair, we look ordinary as the day is long.

Ordinary fucking people. That's us.

My adrenal gland squirts, sudden and cold, as we crest a hill: blue flickering cop rollers up ahead.

"Get in the other lane."

Fredo, white-knuckling the wheel: "That'll look suspicious."

"The hell it will—it's what you're supposed to do."

"Jesus, man. You're getting me all squirrelly."

"Ease over, for fuck's sake."

"When we pass, wave at them."

"I'm not waving at the fucking cops!"

"Nobody up to anything would wave at a cop. It's reverse psychology."

He signals, changes lanes. We pass the cops. Neither of us wave.

I swallow hard: it's not only a trooper but also two black, shiny SUVs with plainclothes narcs standing around—and with a German shepherd, his job apparently now done, panting in the Carolina sunshine. A pair of unhappy campers, spread-eagled against the prowler. Cuffed.

Not hippies—a couple of Latino dudes. Sometimes in the South, or anywhere, really, it helps to look like a middle class whiteboy.

Not a hippy, though. In Reagan-Bush America, hippies get profiled quick as any black dude. Seen it, lived it.

Fredo's Muppet eyes bulge out big and round. "You see that shit?"

The blue lights, growing smaller in the mirror. "They didn't seem to take any notice of us, Captain."

"Screw this. Back road's the way to go."

"Won't that take all day?"

"Won't add but twenty minutes."

"Long as you know where you're going."

"My family's been coming down here all my life, asshat."

❧

A COUPLE of exits later we ditch the great highway. Now we're tooling down a macadam two-lane bumpy with age that gives the suspension on the Lincoln a real workout.

The farther from the interstate we get, the more ramshackle the houses become. Roadside trash, old rusted trucks in weed-choked yards, dead dogs and possums, dirty little kids playing in weedy yards that need cutting. Dudes hanging around in patches of shade outside clapboard country stores. Most of South Carolina is poor like this, my home county included.

We pass a dilapidated, abandoned church, its roof sagging. On the cracked and weathered roadside marquee a few letters still hang:

TRU
G SPEL

"Doesn't that just mean true truth?" In the rural corner of Edgewater County where I'm from, everybody goes to church, including my family, the Lathams. "True truth, true truth, true truth," until the words lose their meaning altogether.

Fredo mumbles, "I think 'gospel' sort of means good news."

"True good news?"

"Man, I dunno. Something like that."

Fredo takes a turnoff onto another band of graying asphalt, one that'll take us right onto the island. The air outside has started to feel humid; the sea and the sawgrass of the marshes await us.

The Dead tape ends, and for a time we ride in quiet.

Finally he says, "That messed with me big-time."

"What?"

"Seeing those dudes get busted."

"What dudes?"

"On the interstate back there."

"Oh—yeah. I hear you."

He's chewing on a thumbnail. "Especially after Hayne, and all. Whoosh."

"Hayne?"

"Well—yeah."

"What about him?"

"After he got popped this summer."

Ice water in my veins. I ask what he means.

He shrugs. "You heard about it. Kind of a big deal."

"Wait—the bust on the island?" The pharmacological super-store. Panic. "*Hayne's the horse trank guy?*"

"Duh. That's why he can't get hold of anything. He's laying low."

"And so now he wants to buy stuff from *us?*"

"Look at the position he's in. Who can he trust?"

"Don't you get it?"

"Bro—get what?"

"Dude's looking at hard time."

Another shrug. "He'll get out of it. Somehow."

"I'll bet he will. With our help."

"Hey—what's that s'posed to mean?"

I explain the situation: that maybe—just maybe—his friend's under pressure from the DEA to pony up fellow drug dealers. Like cops, whether on TV or in real life, always pressure desperate dudes to do.

He's all like, *WHAT?* "Naw, bro."

"Fredo: Think about it."

Plink-plink.

Plink.

"But Tim-bo—his trial's not for months and months. Bro needs money for his lawyer. Says he wants to turn some stuff over fast. That he'll take as much as we have."

"Is that so."

A flicker of uncertainty. "Keeps asking how much we have. How much more we can get." Shakes it off. "Hell, maybe he'll even plea bargain his way out of the whole thing. Meanwhile, he says if we can hook up him regularly, he'll be able to skate through." Nodding and proud. "I'm looking into finding a new source of blow for him back home, too—for weight."

Enough. "You idiot. It's a fucking setup."

At last, a slow sunrise of recognition belies my friend's continued protestation. His voice now comes whiny and small. "But it's Hayne, dude."

I ask Freddie—slowly; carefully—if he even knows what a plea bargain is. How it's obtained.

Fredo literally jams on the brakes and pulls over to the shoulder of the country road. "Party foul."

I'm shaking all over. "Something like that."

Our dust catches up to us and billows into the open windows. Coughing, coughing; cough till you get off, as the saying goes. We both feel the presence of the ECON book, and the doses stashed inside. The sheets. Enough to send us both away for twenty years.

Freddie chews a thumbnail. "When we don't show, Hayne'll get the message."

"He knows how it is with this business."

"When he calls, I'll tell him it's dry. That it's gonna stay that way."

"Now that sounds like a plan."

Freddie, disappointed. "Too bad."

"*Which part?*"

"The beach—it woulda been fun."

"Dude."

Freddie guns that big V-8 cop engine and pulls a U-turn hard enough to make the tires squeal.

Back up to speed, he waxes rhapsodic. "Get home; get wasted. Scope out some hot betties. Watch the game tomorrow. Sling some of these doses to the crunchy campus kids. Friendly faces. Back home we'll be like, safe as kittens."

"Sounds like a plan." Wait—did I say that already?

"You're a fucken broken record, dude."

We cruise by a historical marker, a little turnout with picnic tables; the site of a Revolutionary War incident.

Freddie hits the brakes again, pulls in.

"What now?"

"Maybe we should get stoned."

Realizing about Hayne earlier damn near made me crap myself. "Definitely."

"Not in the car, though."

"Not while we're driving.

Standing beside the marker I hit the Sneak-a-Toke™ and pass it over to Freddie, who cups it in his big hand and holds the smoke in a long time. We talk about the next shows. He says he hopes we catch a "Shakedown Street" on Fall Tour or when we go out to New Year's, but that's three months away. A long time to two college bros with the whole weekend ahead of them, and who still need to get together a headstash.

Five minutes later we're underway again, both of us chewing spearmint gum. Pop in another tape, a jammy second set.

Zipping by another turnout with a historical marker, we both claim to get déjà vu at the same time, and it's like, whoa.

Freddie, laughing and stoned, asks: "Timbo—we still going the right way? Or what?"

Overcome by giggles, all I can do is shrug; if we see the church again, we'll know for sure.

AUTHOR NOTE: A pastiche of events from my college days inspired this rip-snorting tale of two oblivious stoners on a comedic, stormy road to let one deal too many go down. Packed with details observed close at hand as well as at a safe distance, all names have been changed to protect the innocent—kids, don't try this at home. Published in 2017 on Wattpad.com.

THE GOLD ELITE EXPERIENCE

The Harborside Father & Son Forest Fun Run, a good idea gone wrong: it took Chase so long to admit he'd become 'turned around' in the woods—euphemism: lost—he ended up lost indeed. The farther he'd gone, the more the triangular trail blazes had changed from red to a faded and forgotten pinkish hue, until he realized those, too, had vanished.

This part of the red trail must be the dotted segment he'd seen on the map at the trailhead. The leg that hadn't been rendered in a solid line.

Wait—that must mean a future, planned trail.

Of course it did.

Backtracking.

Sighting on the sun.

All to no avail.

All of it the same. Blank birches and thistle bushes and ferns through which he bumbled, their branches scratching his face, arms, shins.

He finally realized maybe the fragrant, heavy foliage meant he'd stumbled close to the river that fed the lake, and bordered the state forest along its northern boundary.

Did the environment suddenly feel more damp?

Was the air cooler?

His chest felt tight.

So alone—more alone than he could recall ever being.

He urinated against a knotty, pale tree. Blasting off bits of peeling, papery bark. Feeling relief.

"Hey." Calling out, zipping up his bulky cargo shorts with pockets full of keys and change. He'd left his phone in the car. Too big. One of those latest models that's halfway to a tablet, it barely fits in a hand, much less pocket. Missing his old iPhone 4S, a slender black monolith of a supercomputer. What could he do? For nearly a year, every time he logged into his phone account the glimmering, golden upgrade icon had been urging him onward. Too much going on. Family bullshit. "Yo. Anybody?"

Nothing in response but birdsong.

This was how people died.

"HEY!"

Echoing and forlorn.

Hearing a squirrel chattering 'angrily,' as he anthropomorphized the nearby rodent in his mind, Chase felt a jolt of fight-or-flight. Squinting up into the dense tree canopy at a patch of blue, he could see a jet aircraft contrail overhead, a fat plume spreading out gauzily across the afternoon sky. The sun, overhead, neither rising nor setting. No direction home, only a spinning spiral and walking a circle in the woods.

Lost.

Missing.

He'd be on the news. Him and his kid. Except the kid would still be alive.

CHASE RESTED ON HIS HAUNCHES, tried to picture the layout of the forest from the map he'd glimpsed on their way into the park —there'd been three or four trails of different colors, including the red dashed one that he thought he'd take to be a little wise guy, certain it eventually crossed another established trail, and hence, a shortcut to win the race and show his kid how awesome dad, mostly absent from the boy's life since the divorce, could be when called upon to do so.

How brilliant it had seemed. Take this alternate path, haul buggy, hup hup hup, then link back up with the goldenrod trail on which the race had started. Emerge with record time. Impressing the kid, and all of them.

Then, he'd gotten mired in angst about the haircut he'd taken that week, and all the trees and needles had begun to look the same, and there weren't any blazes anywhere. No signs to guide.

Shit.

Chase got himself up, brushed off pine needles, and went hunting for the river.

The haircut, brutal.

Markets, up and down.

Ay-yi-yi.

Chase pictured sitting down at the brokerage first thing Monday and ruing the idea. Thinking: You went to work these days and didn't know what numbers were real, and what weren't. You tried not to dwell on the uncertainty of it all. You talked yourself into going out for lunch again, and expensing it again, because who could really keep up anymore? You didn't drink during the day, no, that was some old TV show about madmen. The lunchtime drinkers now were people with problems. They weren't hip. Nowadays, people who drink at lunch go off to rehab. Unless it's day-drinking, of course, which is now a legit thing.

One day downtown he'd watched a couple of hippy kids panhandling, eavesdropping on them talking about how numbers were abstractions. That numbers and words were only 'simulacra of reality,' to use the filthy bum's own inscrutable words. Chase had beamed disapproval and annoyance at the two playing guitars and chanting in the sunshine, with their dirty feet and ridiculous patchwork clothing. Fuck them, he thought. Shut up. You don't matter. If those weren't two drunks, or methheads, or reefer addicts, he'd like to see somebody who was.

The hippy chick smiled and squeezed her eyes like a friendly cat.

Infuriating—they didn't know what work was, what numbers meant, how money and life worked, the sacred symbiosis of it all. Abstractions, his ass.

Complexities? Yeah. That much we got going, Chase said. Complex-er than is possible to explain, if that made sense.

As an insider, though, he went with it. What else was he supposed to do?

Not go into work?

Not trade?

Quit digging for the cheddar?

Declaim that none of the abstractions could possibly add up anymore?

That the bubble of bubbles had to one day pop?

Nobody wanted to hear that. Not even Chase.

THE HARBORSIDE COMMUNITY Chase Ketcham called home represented perhaps the pinnacle of lakeside condo, townhouse and single-family residences in the greater metro area. Closer-in, as the real estate agents would put it, with shorter commutes and convenient to campus and downtown, restaurants, amenities, the beating heart of the small Southern city, sure, you could have all that pizzazz, but in a growing urban environment like the capital city, only for a price. And taking a beating like a rented mule on the ratio of dollars to square footage, too.

However: Out nearer the lake—at least the north side, anyway —those same bucks bought more of everything that could be called desireable, from living space to water to trees to open sky overhead, to stores and restaurants and gyms and car dealerships and yogurt shops. The lakefront offered the sound of the whippoorwills and the sunrises over the dam, and a high general quality of residents who'd purchased or leased within the planned and gated community, insular enough to have developed its own mini-commercial 'town centre' that included a deli, an Irish pub, a dry cleaners, a convenience store (upscale), and most importantly a bank branch, Carolina Trust, which in its familiar logos and cool-blue color scheme Chase found comfort. He had been a customer ever since undergrad, and liked dealing with a locally owned financial institution that represented consistency, stability, familiarity and security in a way the brick edifice of a Wells Fargo branch sitting at the event horizon of Harborside proper could never conjure inside him, though conjure this sensation his community and its little bank did:

If Chase didn't feel at home here at Harborside, he doubted he'd ever feel safe anywhere.

Since the split, he'd suffered a pervasive sensation: losing Janey had been a rug pulled from beneath the stiff, new topsiders he'd worn sockless to the Forest Fun Run, shoes that had rubbed stinging red blisters on both his pinky toes, two of a growing number of oozing, open wounds.

Nitwit.

The loss still ached. You talk about haircuts and abstractions —Janey, that one, tough to quantify. To process.

Especially with the kid.

After the divorce, moving out to his townhouse here in Harborside, an attempt to reboot, just a little farther from Herndon Hill back downtown where he'd lived for most of his adult life. Too many mutual friends. Too many chances to see his ex with the new fuckbuddy.

It was more serious than that, though, which was the worst part. *Stepdad* had entered the vernacular of their boy.

Chase didn't like it. Not one bit. Daddy was daddy, and as had been discussed at length around the (former) family dinner table, would remain so.

Haircut of haircuts, the whole breakup with Janey. All of it.

And with the quarter going the way it was going, Chase felt ready to punt. Or to grunt—grunt one out. A big relieving cathartic psychic dump.

Nah. He just needed more cheddar.

~

TO WIT: Harborside was affordable but not cheap—what is, anymore?—and his own boy was growing up. Ten this year, a little man on the cusp of bigger-littlemandom. Next thing, the little shit would be car shopping.

Getting caught screwing, smoking dope, dealing painkillers or steroids, if the tyke got into sports.

Worse? Matriculating. Wanting to go out of state. Or Ivy League.

Jesus.

Money. That's what it all meant.

Moe Munny, that's who Chase needed to get next to. Oh yeah. Not his ex-wife, nor Jason's stepfather or whatever he was to think of the one-eyed snake of a usurper who'd taken away Chase's old family life. Ugh. Like taking a knock to the nasties, that part.

All of it.

How she'd put it to him: Unfulfilling. A mistake. Et cetera.

Nice.

Moe Munny was the answer, though, and Chase needed to get that a-hole on speed-dial. Yeah, he did. Needed some luck and positive thinking and no more haircuts for a while. Of any kind, whether financial or otherwise.

Moe Munny make it all better. It was like what Chase's hotel reward-points program used for a tagline:

Once You've Enjoyed the Gold Elite Experience, You'll Never Again Settle for Less.

~

HARBORSIDE FATHER & Son Forest Fun Run. Something—anything—to do with the little meathead on their weekend together.

Whose bright idea, this?

Should've listened to the boy.

"Slicing not slapping." A week ago, Chase gurgling through a throat of chlorine as he sliced along; Jason, dangling sausage legs in the shallow end of the country club pool. Chase, a swimmer in high school—for half a season—had thought this activity, making some chop in the olympic-size cement pond, would burn babyfat off the both of them.

"See? Slicing."

"Yeah, Dad. Right." Jason, sliding into the water and splashing around like a kid instead of a competitive swimmer. "Slicing—like baloney."

"Swim over here. You gotta get your heart rate up."

"Heart rate." Drawing it out. "I'm gonna get right on that."

So dismissive. Just like her. Jason also looked like his mom, only a foot shorter and twice as round.

Chase, he'd been the one blindsided. Had wondered for how long before the separation and eventual divorce the fuckbuddy'd been in the picture.

She'd said nah, nah, no way, dude: Rather than engaging in current activity, which Chase had sputtered and insisted had to be the reason, she only wanted out to have the *opportunity* to do other dudes. Well, that made it better.

Liar—what a liar she'd been.

What'd it matter now? Chase had gotten laid plenty, before and after the divorce. He didn't care. Couldn't afford to—this asshole had haircuts and issues and all manner. Of *schtuff*. To deal with.

Thinking about it all on the turnaround in the pool made him suck water. Feeling like an idiot, he surfaced coughing and gagging, his stroke and pace irrevocably broken.

Flinging his hair like a wet dog, Chase floated and squinted across the pool for his son. He watched his boy drifting on his back, his belly forming a small fleshy island. Jason splashed away with little circular motions of his wrists, and at a pretty good clip. Chase bobbed.

TOWELING off in the locker room, he'd read the Fun Run flyer, a(nother) chance for bonding and growth.

"This is perfect for us, champ. We both need to get into decent shape. No better way than to run off that flab."

Jason, skepticism leaning to mistrust. "Shouldn't we get into shape before we go for a freaking *run*, though? That's what I think we ought to do. Let's stick with the pool. Don't you think? I do."

He'd inherited his mother's debating style—ask a question, don't wait for someone else's answer.

"We're in fine shape. It's a jog in the forest. I'll sign us up." Chase had scanned the QR code from the flyer, which opened up a registration form in his browser. "We'll get ourselves a couple pairs of New Balances, and we'll be off. Like The Flash."

Jason pulled on husky-sized shorts that reached halfway down his calves. "Nobody cares about The Flash. Have you seen that *Justice League* trailer? His costume looks stupid."

Chase ground his gears, wondering if there were a newer super-fast superhero, perhaps from the Marvel universe rather than DC, whom Jason would admire more. Once they got settled into the car, he'd google it on the phone. That's how you kept up with a kid like this. But only after registering them for the run.

In the car: "I don't want to do the Fun Run."

"Of course *you don't have to*, son. But I'm asking you to."

"I thought swimming was supposed to get us into better shape."

"That, too. Running—jogging, I mean; easy does it—and swimming. Both."

"Nah. I don't wanna. Forget it."

"Well, you're gonna."

"Thought I didn't have to."

"Changed my mind."

"No."

"Son—I'm insisting."

Jason sighed. A sidelong glance. "All right, father. I'll go along with your little fun run scheme." But only this time, his eyes—his mother's—seemed to say. "Sure I will."

"This'll be great. Get away from town, out in the woods. Maybe we'll start going camping. Would you dig that, kid?"

"Fun Run. Camping." He punched through Chase's saved satellite radio channels, snorting in disgust at each one. "Sounds great."

THE MORNING OF THE HF&SFFR, the lake beyond the townhouse patio lay glassy and silver under a puffy, unsettled sky like ashy cotton candy. As Chase stretched his quads and waited for Jason to finish his breakfast and bathroom biz, the surface of the water rippled like a vast sheet of slate-colored, textured highthread count bed sheet, and it was all so much like the overwrought description in a boring short story in the back half of a literary journal bleeding print subscribers season by season and barely hanging on that Chase made himself stop thinking about how the lake looked.

Instead, he stretched his calves, and did a few deep-knee bends. It hurt, really hurt. Swimming had been hard on his knees.

His dad had told him to swim instead of going out for track. "Hard on the joints," his old man had said. "Beat your joints to death hoofing around that track every day." So Chase hadn't gone out for track, had swum instead. Yet here he staggered with the lousy aching knees anyway. Fucked over coming and going.

As the Fun Run had gotten underway, Chase felt winded—nobody'd mentioned the incline you hit almost immediately, hard packed dirt leading into the deep woods past the info kiosk with the trail maps, the colorful lines, most solid but one large looping link broken and dotted. Despite the searing pain in both lungs, he lurched ahead.

Like a couple of other dads with chubby sons, at first he'd hung back with his boy, thinking maybe Jason had been right. That neither of them were in shape for this damn thing. Yet here they were.

"Jesus, Dad," his boy called, hoofing it along the dirt trail, falling behind. "I'm gonna puke."

"Just gotta shake it off. Hup hup."

But after a couple minutes his topsiders grew heavy, and he wanted to puke, too. No showing that to Jason, though, or to any of the other boys or dads. A leader had to lead.

Effortless, light-footed, and mocking of expression, a pair of long-legged teens, limber and lean, glided by the knot of slower fun-runners. Smartasses. Like Chase had been, fifty pounds and twenty years ago.

"Look." One of them, cocking an elbow at Jason. "It shakes just like a great big bowl of jelly."

"Ho-ho-ho," the other one chimed in.

"Hey, Beavis." Chase, winded but threatening. "That's my kid you're talking about."

"We meant you, dipshit," the first wiseass called back.

"Hey—" Chase made a pathetic lunge at catching up. "Eff you."

Chortling, they kicked into a fifth gear and zoomed away into the hardwoods like the speeder-bikes in *Star Wars*, the one with the teddy bears at war on the forest planet.

Chase eased back and huffed alongside Jason for a bit, but his longer legs invariably took him ahead of the pack, especially as those slower boys had all stopped running and begun walking.

A burning sensation trickled down his left arm. But he ran. Faster. He had to show the boys how it was done.

Getting a second wind. "Hup hup," he yelled one last time.

His mind, suddenly bright and clear. A feeling of limitless energy flowed through him. Got the big idea about the fork he thought led to the shortcut on the map, the red dotted loop-around. He set the gearshift for the high gear of his soul. Ran.

His mind had wandered. Along with the rush of the endor-phins, a thousand different thoughts sneaking in. Threads of his life—work, the divorce, the kid. The future.

Trying to grab hold of the future. Wrangling those numbers.

Predictive programming. That's what he desired. No more surprises.

Desire flooded into him. He ran harder.

The woods became dense and unfamiliar, and then the trail split and the gold triangle blazes had given way to the red ones, and he went with his gut and angled left, then the red faded to pink. Then no markers at all. And lost.

His mind, a wreck.

HE FINALLY STOPPED WANDERING, took another piss—all the Starbucks—and began worrying about dehydration. Took a breather. Got his bearings.

Walked. And walked.

Doubling, tripling back had done no good. The backs of the trees held no triangles to find. Seeing the same trees, over and over. Brambles and briars and undergrowth, way far off the mani-cured state forest trail.

Calling out.

Silence. And walking.

An hour passing. The Fun Run, over by now.

Were they looking for him?

Had they signed in like you were supposed to?

No—they'd been late. They'd driven into the State Forest parking lot amidst all the other sedans and SUVs, gotten out and gone straight into the run. No one knew they were out there. No record.

The forest, enormous. Chase could die.

Maybe this was how it was to be. Alone and forgotten.

Did it matter? Jason, a stepdaddy lined up.

Chase could disappear among the trunks and limbs and ferns and peat of the forest floor, the loamy underfloor of leaves and needles and decay, and it wouldn't matter. He was already dead and moldering. He'd fit right in.

BUT IN A BLAZE OF INTUITION, Chase took a chance on a hunch and found an older trail not part of the state forest layout, a well-trodden dogleg that angled down a steep drop to the blessed muddy riverbank. Now he knew he'd be able to get his bearings— a long way from the entrance to the forest, but escape could now be had. The river only flowed one way.

Thing was: did he want to escape this place?

He sat and pondered.

He slurped a handful of water from the river—a foolish idea. Who knew what was discharged upstream? But the water, running clear through this deep channel. He drank some more, and damn if it didn't taste clean and sweet.

He sat. Allowed his mud to settle.

Thought about death, and the fear he felt.

About being versus nonbeing.

Caught sight of a yellow flower out of the corner of his eye, then many of them, all up and down the riverbank. Flowers, yellow and beautiful and tiny, as though they'd opened just for Chase.

Abstractions.

And yet, all this here in the woods, by the river? The flowers, they felt real. Realer than real.

Thought about leaving it all behind.

It = the numbers.

Dropping his shoulders, he relaxed his posture. A kink under his left clavicle flared. Grunting with effort, he reached around and massaged the muscle best he could. It felt better.

He stretched out his tired legs—the tissues were jumping—and pointed his big toes toward the river, flexing his calves, an old stretch he used to do beside the pool to lubricate all the joints of the legs, ankles all the way up to the hip flexors. Kicked off the topsiders that had rubbed blisters on his feet, which were redder than newborn mice.

He relaxed into this pose.

Chase rested.

Quieted his mind.

Time, turning elastic.

SNAPPING out of a near sleep-like fugue state, he felt a moment of crystalline clarity like the earlier rush. All the numbers had dropped away. He visualized the data. Said, these data are abstractions.

Afterwards, he shoved away his desire to shove the numbers away. And left all-but nothing. Till he stopped thinking about nothing.

He rested anew.

The thought came: he could say 'no.' To what it didn't seem to matter. 'No.' Or else: yes. But yes only to what he wanted. To what felt right and true.

The thought felt circular.

A blue pulsing light formed behind his eyelids. A blue eye on a vast yellow background, watching him. Strange dream, he thought.

His eyes opened again. Observed water flowing over a particular rock, one mostly submerged and rounded smooth, a couple of inches of clear river rippling across its surface like a standing wave that flickered in and out of frequency with itself.

A frequency like eternity. The rock and the river, outlasting him.

Outlasting the numbers themselves.

Chase splashed the cool river onto his face. Stood up and stretched and yawned and felt new as the day was long.

Being in the woods, lost, had seemed to cleanse Chase of all sorts of notions and troubles and of time slipping away. And of numbers. It would be summer, soon, and Jason would be out of school and spending the whole time with him here at Harborside. They'd walk the forest together—no need to run.

AT LAST HE began to hike his way out, along the river at first, then angling in at the right point to meet back up with the goldenrod trail he remembered as ending near a boat landing downstream, where snacks and juice boxes had awaited the dads and sons, and where he hoped there would still be somebody—anybody—looking for him.

But if they weren't looking, at least he still had himself.

He didn't hurry. He didn't feel as though there was anywhere to be, or anywhere to get to.

That would change—he knew it would, soon as he saw another person, much less got back to the car and checked his phone and turned on the radio in time for the news at the top of the hour. Then, the drive back to the townhouse, and the groceries that needed to be bought, and the dropping Jason off with his mom bit, with stilted small talk with or about her new beau, and all of this would come to a head late Sunday night as he tried to drift away into gentle sleep, rest that felt different from what'd happened beside the river.

Maybe he'd sit in quietude out at the lake later, as he had by the river. Maybe he'd do it every day. Hell—twice a day.

"*Dad,*" a voice echoed in the distance. "*Hey.*"

Grinning, Chase cupped his mouth: "Hey, kidlet—over here."

A rustling of the huge ferns and dry leaves underfoot. His boy, calling out: "What the eff? Everybody's looking for you."

"Over here by the river. C'mon this way."

Jason sounded closer, but only a little. "No way—you come to me."

"Way!" the father exhorted. "Come and see the river. Watch the water rush rippling over these big, smooth stones. And sit and think about nothing with me. It's amazing."

AUTHOR NOTE: A comedic meditation on getting back to nature and quieting the mind—on meditating, in other words—the simple fable offered by 'The Gold Elite Experience' previously appeared online at Wattpad.com. Trivia: the wry, winking character name 'Chase Ketcham' is recycled from an early set of unpublished linked stories called 'Blackwater River.'

FIVE O'CLOCK SOMEWHERE

I 've been trying to get up earlier these days—four o'clock, four-thirty at the latest.

In the afternoon.

That's working the vampire shift for ya.

Before daylight savings time ends, which is next weekend, I want to enjoy a taste of each day's fleeting sunshine. Once the Carolina autumn sets in, and the sky turns dark in the late afternoon? I'll feel as though I've missed the whole day, other than what I might get to see walking home from the bar after work, amidst the waking world going about its business. I'll admit I've been at this long enough now that I feel unstuck and out of place among the worker bees, whose lives unfold bathed in the light of the life-giving sun.

Suckers.

The night time's the real time.

The only time. At least since they invented electricity.

And especially tonight, the Eve of All Saints, sure to be a memorable time slinging suds. Just another night to me. Another shift.

PADDY, who's been in the bar trade long enough to know, took me aside the other day, offered to rotate with me and work graveyard for a few weeks.

He said, "Casey, I've been watching you. Your game is off. Your electrolytes seem imbalanced. You need plentiful fresh air and some naturally occurring Vitamin D. Trust me."

At first I reckoned Vitamin D to mean some old guy's brand of speed from the 70s or early 80s, back before they had cocaine. Said so.

He laughed. Said he meant a normal life, lived during the daylight. "This bar trade—the vampire shift, anyway—it's in abeyance with the natural order of things."

"And yet you keep pouring."

"Pays the bills here on the big plantation, pal. And too late to learn another line. Anyway. Offer's good, whenever you're ready."

"I'll keep it in mind."

"You should. You got circles under your eyes, like the undead."

Paddy opens the bar every day, stocks, cleans, maintains and slings during happy hour, where he has his loyal crowd. He makes good tips, is locally famous—or else infamous—for a deceptively potent, layered build he calls the Paddywhacker, not really much different from Long Island iced tea. Worked in half the dives around here, going all the way back to the 70s, he says. Paddy, a bartender's bartender. A pro, unlike me.

But I told him, nah, I'm into the groove, and so I think for now I'll keep things as they are. I make decent scratch working the late shift. He knows that. Doesn't give a shit about my pale complexion—he probably needs the bucks. Girlfriend's at least two or three decades younger than him.

Doesn't matter. I'm not long for this trade. My photography's bound to come into focus soon, haha, and get the juices kick-started and a career underway, finally. Or hell, maybe go to grad school.

In any case, I'll soon be done with the bar life. I'm on the windward side of 30. Something better happen one of these days —right? After all, it's not like I'm a professional bartender. Not like Paddy.

MORE I THINK ABOUT IT, he probably does care about my well-being. That's the kind of guy Paddy is: crusty but empathetic, a good listener, wisdom at the ready no matter the subject. He's also more sensitive than most folks know, more worldly. Reads poetry like Yeats, Blake, Rilke, Wallace Stevens. Much much more to this guy than just some aging dude slinging liquor. He went to South-eastern, he said. Was an English major.

Dude's so real I once saw him cry, back when we got the news that old Rogers Cuthbert had died. Rogers, he'd been a regular at the Parlor for as long as anyone could remember, and I don't mean on Friday afternoons—five, six days a week, slurping down gin and tonics, Marlboro Light menthols smoldering between those gnarled yellow knuckles of his. A regular's regular. Like the sunrise. Clockwork.

For a solid week after we heard, we kept his high-backed chair at the corner tilted forward so no one could sit there, and on the bar where his drink would have been? We placed a single red rose in a vase—on a coaster—and watched the petals fade and turn brown around the edges, the way people do, the way Rogers had done: before our very eyes.

Cancer, someone told us. I'd noticed the weight coming off, but he never said a word about being sick. Was always good old irascible, sardonic Rogers, and this despite dying day by day. Staring it down. Like everyone, I guess, if you want to take his worldview, which was cynical at best.

One night when he was leaving I asked: "Rogers, look here."

"What?"

"How come you sit greasing this bar with those knobby elbows every night?"

"Why the fuck you want to ask me a question like that?"

I said because there were plenty of other joints in the neighborhood.

A Members Only windbreaker in Southeastern Redtails burgundy went on over bony shoulders. "Ain't to sit here looking at Paddy's ugly mug. Or yours either, for that matter. That's for goddamn sure."

I asked what, then.

"The minty-fresh stink of the urinal pucks. That's what keeps me coming back. In fact, order me a case so's I can give them out at Christmas."

I would say he gave me a wink, or that his eyes smiled, but it wasn't that way. I didn't cry over him. Rogers wasn't 'my' regular. He belonged to Paddy.

PADDY and I work in a true bartender's bar. The Parlor, despite its folksy sounding name, is the principal late-night joint in the college ghetto they call the Old Market, down the hill from sprawling Southeastern University, with its roiling burgeoning student population numbering in the tens of thousands. I probably don't have to tell you that we have over thirty bars in a four-block commercial district.

Here's our real niche at the Parlor: every night is SIN night. Here, we offer Crappy Hour, which lasts from three in the *ayeem* until five. This is the time when other service industry prols at all the other bars count down, clean, close up and make their way over here to hang out in our dim nooks, on the leather couches perfect for semiprivate assignations, or clustered along our long burnished bar top Paddy keeps impeccable and polished, upon which other assignations are also said to have occurred; or else out back on the porch facing the alley, where, if one's inclined, it's possible to take a discreet toke or two, bearing in mind that every so often the heat rolls through, trying to maintain a modicum of social order here in the wild east.

Ah, the back porch—a fine place for customers and bartenders alike to sit unobserved on empty kegs and get high, to receive a sequestered and secret hummer from a drunken acquaintance, or else to avoid the mindless drunken prattle and general air of hustling inside. Or perhaps to talk in hushed tones for hours with a girl, a special one in whom you've found what you at last perceive as genuine love beyond the boundaries of mere hormonal compulsion, until her beauty seeps into your mind and continues for years to haunt your dreams.

Poetic. I shoulda considered being an English major.

The Parlor doesn't know of endings, like relationships that've gone sour; the Parlor doesn't even have a posted closing time. If the Parlor wants to, it can stay open until ten in the morning.

If 'it' wants to, eh? The bar, with a will of Its own to boot? The Parlor has a vibe and a flow and a rhythm, yes, but a will? Highly doubt that, though the place is said to feature a ghost or two, not that I've seen. Save these notions of personification for the English majors like my ex, Becca.

Not that Becca, and who she was to me, matters now. In fact, if I don't get moving this morning—this evening, rather—I'm liable to start clicking around on Facebook looking for her. I won't find her anyway, because she never had time to fuck around online like most people seem to.

BREAKFAST OF CHAMPS, nom nom nom, procured at the Markette Diner two blocks from the Parlor, all of it walking distance from my crib up the hill.

The Markette, a godsend, serves such meals twenty-four-seven; it might sound crazy, but I've both started and ended shifts hunched at its Formica counter gnawing charred meat. Character.

History. It's a part of the larger fabric of the Old Market, this joint, so much so that its name suggests this symbiotic relationship.

My entree of choice for Halloween is called Hangover Hash-browns, one popular with the late night bar crowd, or any time of the day: it's a couple of runny, over easy eggs flopped on top of potatoes grilled with onions, sweet peppers, and sharp cheddar cheese, all fried up on the ancient blackened griddle. The food is salted once by the cook, and again by me. Toast. A slice of navel orange. A big platter.

Like everything on the menu, the plate represents a hell of a good deal for the money. Students, they need to make the dollars stretch. Students, post-grads, other unreconstructed, devolved adolescents unable to move on from the besotted milieu of their storied and youthful adventures.

Whoa, whoa, whoa—spoiler space. I can see myself reflected in the tines of my fork that scrapes at the last of the grease. A dangling tendril of cheese more orange than nature intended. A stray sweet banana pepper. Shredded potatoes dripping oil. Carbs to fuel the long night ahead.

Larry the cook, holding a blackened spatula he grips with tension. "Something wrong with ya food?"

"Nothing, dude. Spacing out."

"You looking at that fork like it fixing to talk to you."

"Just trying to decide if I want the last bite."

"Who don't want the last bite?" Saying it like it ought to have fifteen question marks. But not funny like in a comedy. More like scared at the thought of the uneaten last morsel on a plate of his food. Larry, he thinks I'm crazy. He thinks the world is crazy. He's told me as much.

I eat the food.

Larry, he takes my plate away. Cook, server, busboy, all in one; it's a small lunch counter. "Mo' coffee?"

"Thanks—that was righteous." Leaning into it. "*Every bite.*"

"Appreciate it." The sound of the coffee dribbling into the

stained china, a standard white diner cup. At only four ounces, you need it refilled. A lot.

"Dude, you deserve it. You make that grill sing."

Repeating in a monotone, no eye contact: "Appreciate it."

Paddy says Larry has short-order cooked at about every place there's been around these parts. One of those bartender exaggerations. Paddy, he's served enough booze to float the fleet, as he puts it. Language. Style. Larry could use some.

I'm struck that he and I seem like the only folks not wearing some get-up. "So, Larry—who you supposed to be tonight?"

"Say what, now?"

I gesture at two *Star Wars* characters walking by the open front door, at two other kids sitting in one of the booths—the girl's a fairy with gossamer wings, her date a Latin lover in a shiny zoot suit, wearing a fake plastic pompadour with phony bling hanging around his neck.

"Costumes? Ya dig?"

"Oh—fuck that noise." He goes back to the griddle, another pile of onions and potatoes sizzling in a puddle of grease. Larry slashes at a sizzling lump of meat. Mumbling, annoyed to the point of anger. "No sir, not me. Bunch of damn fools."

I'm pleased. "We kids, or what?"

"Kids?"

Lowering my voice. "Playing dress-up."

"Word to that." Grease popping, he worries the hash browns with his spatula. "Ain't playing no dress-up."

On my way out I nod to the couple, cheeseburger condiments dripping from their fingers. They don't notice me. A sly sweet smile as she reaches across and slurps two good swallows of his chocolate shake.

She glances at me. Her expression changes to one of concern, pulling me out of my trance.

As I trudge off to work, the violence of their quiet intimacy haunts and confounds me.

~

I CRUISE into the Parlor to find a few regulars sipping beers, classic rock on the satellite channel which I'll later change to 90s hits, an air of calm before the storm. Scattered folks loll and lounge in the booths along the walls with the small televisions a patron can tune to any number of channels. Only one person in the whole place is in costume: a guy made up like classic Lugosi Dracula. All the others are in normal garb, which comes as no small relief.

But tension's in the air. Paddy cuts narrowed eyes at me and the far end of the bar where the big bossman, Reed 'Reedy' Giordano, sits yapping into his mobile and gesticulating; Reedy, a hand-talker, like a magician practicing misdirection. He leans on the bar, looking as though he hasn't a care in the world.

I cruise by the bossman, nod.

He ends his call, eyeballs me in silence.

I hang up my jacket, nodding to the aging hippy dude, Neill. Like Rogers Cuthbert, Neill drinks in here from four until about nine pretty much every night of the week but Sunday. That's when he's off doing old hippie shit, I guess. Tending his mushroom crops. Whatever they do when they go to ground.

"Hey now, bossman."

Reedy asks me what's shaking. Calls me 'big-time.'

An odd smell in the air, like sulphur. "Paddy, you got a sour stomach again?"

Paddy grunts a non-answer, keeps slicing limes into a pile of shiny green chunks. "Be glad I'm doing this side work for you."

My boss cocks his head. Gets that certain twinkle in his eye, the ball-busting sort. "So what you supposed to be for Halloween? Aging fratboy with a gut?"

Everybody in earshot goes hardy-har.

"I don't do costumes."

"Coulda fooled me."

"Besides, bossman—what about you?"

"I got this crazy werewolf mask out in the Beemer, ugly as hell. Big bloody tongue hanging out." He mimes the tongue with three wriggling, downturned fingers. "Looks like some goddamn demented Wiley E. Coyote. Got it at Halloween Express over by the Wallyworld."

Paddy asks, "Hitting up a party?"

"Nah. Just gonna scare the crap outta my kids."

What a psycho—his kids are like, one and three. "Reedy, I dunno. I had an uncle pull that kind of crap on me. You'll scar them for life, dude."

"So that's what your problem is? Scarred for life by childhood trauma?"

"All right. So what'd I do?"

His eyes flare Budweiser red from a neon sign behind the bar. "You tell me."

"You're really riding me tonight, bossman."

Scoffing. "Grow a pair, you pussy."

My cheeks grow hot. His vitriol renders me mute. "—"

Reedy's phone buzzes but he ignores the call, dropping the black device into his jacket pocket. "Now, I don't know what goes on around here when you're shutting down. If you have friends hanging out, girls, whatever. Ain't like I don't know how this business goes. But lookit, I don't like the inventory sheets. Something ain't right."

"What does 'something' mean?"

"Numbers don't feel right."

"I ain't skimming, chief."

"Hope not."

"Reedy—you know me."

"Nobody knows anybody. Not really."

"C'mon, bossman."

Now one of the other bartenders, Kaylee, looking puffy-eyed, appears out of the back room. Kaylee's been here a long time now too, five years. She works a couple shifts a week, also as a server in a wings joint downtown in the other nightlife district.

She's high maintenance and sensitive to criticism, but on the other hand does a good job, seems honest, and probably hates Reedy's interrogation as much as I do. Twenty-seven, Kaylee's chubby-cute; since starting to work here, she's put on weight (said Mr. Pot Kettleblack). Kaylee's always griping about men. She's been through a raft of loser guys. I hear it all from her, twice a week, clockwork.

Last year she confessed having to get an abortion, a saga confided to me through drunken tears one morning around daybreak, and after numerous shots of Jäger. Teary, bitter. How the guy had done the right thing by paying for the procedure, and all? But like, how he'd never called her again, for which she was both glad but also sad in some vague way? I felt bad, but could think of no comfort to offer other than another shot, a lingering hug on the sidewalk, both of us blinking back morning sun far too hot and bright for our incipient hangovers to tolerate. I had thought the night about to end with the two of us finally in bed together. Not after that story.

"Anyway." Reedy waves Kaylee and me both over to him. "This is a good crew here. Let's keep it that way—noses clean. All that jazz."

"I think it was that way before, honestly. But, yeah, boss. Of course."

Those red eyes, they pierce me. "You guys seem like you really love this place."

I offer a hearty handshake. "Like a second home to me."

Reedy's taken aback for some reason, appears ruminative. A word like Becca might have used. I tried to work on my vocabulary because of her, but the odd part? It's that I waited to do so until after she'd left.

The boss goes out to his car parked illegally in the alley, like he always parks—the important guy, flouting the rules. Who's gonna fuck with him?

I don't know, maybe he's earned such a privilege. He's got other businesses, owns a couple of buildings. Prosperous. He started with the Parlor, though. Made his first money right here. Close to his heart, he says. No wonder he keeps an eye on the joint.

"Thank god." Kaylee blows out her lips. "Prick."

With that weird energy dissipated, I get my apron on and dance fingers across the speedrails to make sure we're stocked with plenty of house liquors, the Beams and Smirnoffs. The call brands, they're all displayed behind me on tiered lighted platforms, a warm aesthetic touch, more classy than the Parlor probably deserves. Mixers, garnishes—all stocked up. Paddy. What a pro.

"What'd he say to you?"

Petulant. "All but accused me of skimming. What bullshit. Fuck him."

"Are you?"

Kaylee, mortified. "*Am I what?*"

"Skimming. What did you think I meant?"

A laugh. "Hell, no." She puts on a set of furry pink kitty cat ears, pulls out a compact. She draws whiskers on her cheeks with an eyebrow pencil.

"Meow. Here, pussy-pussy."

Flips me off. "Where's your costume?"

I explain my rectitude about participating in the ritualistic donning of occult-themed finery, of toying around with my own familiar markers of identity, concluding with a platitude regarding the pretentiousness of pretending: "Everyone should be satisfied with who they are."

"Loser," making the L with her kitty-cat thumb and forefinger. "C'mon, it's fun."

"Not for me."

"You're what my grandmother called a wet blanket."

"Hang me out to dry, then."

Concern. "Your banter—it's forced. What's wrong, hon?"

I shake my head, go on about my business.

~

I TELL Paddy that since I'm here he should knock off; he's all over the idea like stink on shit, gone baby gone.

He'd been quiet and cold to us both; I suppose maybe that Paddy's the source of Reedy's suspicion, but in this case they're both wrong. Scottie, who comes in later, represents another possibility, but I think his sins begin and end with being stoned as a bat a hundred freaking percent of the time.

The deep, smokescarred voice of Hippy Neill, in his literal cups of heavy brown ale, gets my shift off to a comforting start as he regales a few folks with one of his standard bits, a story I've heard a couple dozen times if I've heard it once—but hey, it's Neill, he tips out real good, and so he gets to sit and tell all the stories he wants.

Tonight he's made some new friends, kids who never got to go to a Dead show because they were too young. This makes Neill a kind of pop culture oral historian, the type you find in bars like this one.

"—and so it's like, we had dosed a good solid hour before we left the house, right? And this shit, they called it windowpane— little amber gel tabs," squinting and making a tiny shape with thumb and forefinger. "This acid was like white lightning." Shrugging, laughing. "I mean god-dog, man. I'm talking break you down into your component parts, all the way down to the molecular level, and put you back together. And that's just in the first set of the show."

At this point in the telling he flutters his hand around and bulges his eyes, trying to mime the onset of the psychedelic. "So anyways," he continues, fluttering, "we're off to the show, it's like the good old Grateful Dead, and they're gonna be right here in the goddurn Coop," the university's venerable basketball arena. "You can't get your mind around it, but it's all good. Everybody dosed, all of us riding piled up in the back of my boy Tommy's shit Suburban. Man, that heap had so many Dead stickers on the back window you couldn't see out."

"A cop magnet," one of the young dudes says.

"True that. But you *could* see out the sides, and we was keeping an eye for them old bacon-burgers. We was tripping, and young, watching the world pass by. It felt like one of the greatest nights of my life coming on, not just another acid trip." Neill goes faraway, like one of the Dead's deep jams. "I could see the road ahead, and it was golden."

One of the kids says, "Whoa."

"But then," Neill's voice turning dark, "dang if we don't take this back street? The one that runs over yonder past Hubert Maxwell Park. And what's next to that?"

I goose the story along. "Isn't the Southeastern ROTC mini-campus over there?"

"Ding, ding, ding." Neill slaps the bar with an open palm, star-tling his rapt audience of three. "Damn straight it is."

Neill goes on to relate how they saw these ROTC cadets all lined up in full camo with their rifles and a couple of jeeps. How his buddy Russell James, freaked at the sight of the military machines, started screaming, "Something ain't right, man, *some-thing ain't right, man.*" Neill says this big punchline a few times in this high, panicky voice, laughing so hard tears squirt out and he has to catch his breath. "Something ain't right," he wheezes one last time, barely able to breathe it's so goddamn funny.

He goes on to explain how he had to talk his buddy down. Persuade him that martial law hadn't been declared because of the Grateful Dead or nuclear war or Martians landing or what-ever. "I tell y'all what, we still say that to each other to this very day, me and old Russell James. 'Something ain't right, man!' God almighty, if that's not funny as hell," raising his ale like the Statue of Liberty, "*then I don't know what is.*"

Neill, giving me a wink, takes the kids up on an offer of a round of shots, including one for me. I pour myself a JD neat.

Toss it back and chase with ice water, like some hard-case, hard-drinking private eye in a movie on TV.

My stomach convulses.

My throat burns.

A little early for it.

Neill, out of stories, settles up and tips 25 percent before staggering out to his van parked in one of the angled spaces out front along the main drag. I don't worry about him driving home—he lives nearby, a few blocks. Probably, like me, by design. Why he drives here, I don't know. Some folks, they court trouble.

WE GET A POP. Like they dropped off a busload. Costumes, revelry. We change the music from my 90s hits to dance party EDM.

The drinks flow. Floor getting sticky, hands too, but between orders I keep them rinsed, especially after rounds with syrupy ingredients.

For a solid hour Kaylee and I work side by side—a machine, a delicate dance. It's nothing but a blur of slinging liquor and pulling heavy, heady draught beer with foam that Kaylee says reminds her of the beaches down in Charleston, where she went with her last boyfriend all the time and the foam's all brown from the freighter traffic.

Sounds ridiculous, her nostalgia. She hadn't gone out with that guy more than two months.

An older dude, no costume, in his late 30s and out of place, asks if I'll change the music to jamband or classic rock.

I tell him to forget it. "We decide on the music."

"Eat a deuce," flinging a pair of aggressive fingers at me like he's in a hip-hop video and I'm the camera. "Buddy-row," he adds, his eyes dancing with intoxication.

I have no idea what the deuce he's taking about. I signal the doorman with a green laser pointer, a tipoff that we've got a soused one on the loose, but the drunk staggers off on his own, out of the bar and on his way.

After the pop abates, the Parlor's steady but not packed, which is a surprise since it's Halloween, though granted it is a Tuesday and not a good weekend night like you want for a national drinking holiday such as this one. Besides, most bars have costume contests and other such bullcrud.

At the Parlor?

We drink, read, talk about important stuff. We peak late, and on our own terms.

~

PEAK EXPERIENCES?

Like with Becca?

There's her booth, the only two-top along the wall, tucked into the corner on the other side of the entrance. Empty, a pool of pale light illuminating the spot where she used to sit reading, highlighting text, her glasses slipping down her nose.

Becca.

The girl who didn't order cocktails, who instead studied while drinking our lousy, weak iced tea—doing her work here, she said, because in the coffee shops she always ran into people she knew and never got enough done. Becca, smoking, reading, looking bookish, whatever that means, which to me meant beautiful. Nodding to me as I'd come in for my shift, early, back when I worked as Paddy's backup and got off about midnight.

When she started calling and texting me instead of the other way around? I would get butterflies in my stomach, like back in sixth grade when I was in love with Staci MacDougal from down the street, would try to screw up enough courage to sit beside her on the bus.

Becca. We hung out. We went out. We stayed over, made breakfast together. Started sitting other places besides the bar, neither trading in witty flirtatious repartee nor often having conversations at all. Just being together.

It felt like love.

To me, anyway.

A SENSE-MEMORY: a slow night spent watching her study, which she said she enjoyed, my attention from across the bar. Looking at Becca's face, an easy task, even all twisted up by working on a paper about literary post-postmodernism.

Understanding neither pomo nor post-pomo, I asked for an example.

Her eyebrows elevated, a weird flat smile. "*Infinite Jest?* Something that goes beyond self-referential, into a state of what you might call meta-meta?"

"Oh, right. I got you." The hell I did.

I told her about how this cat I knew named Herbie used a copy of *Infinite Jest* as a prop, carrying a thick, well-thumbed and highlighted copy of the novel in order to strike up conversations with what Herbie called 'brainiac types.'

Despite being his term and not mine, she still frowned in distaste. Complained that what I'd said constituted a "pejorative hitting a little close to home."

"That's Herbie talking. Not me."

"Did he actually read the book?"

"Herbie? Never read a word. Not that I saw."

"Did it work? His little prop?"

Shrugging. "Sometimes."

"What a loser."

"Who? Herbie, or the brainiac who fell for his line?"

Becca scowled and shifted gears. "I feel guilty. I'm referencing David Foster Wallace, but honestly?" She put her hands over her mouth. Her cheeks reddened. "I couldn't finish it."

"Why not?"

"Gave up under the weight of the footnotes."

I didn't know what *Infinite Jest* was like or what role footnotes played, only that the novel was long, and how I'd never attempt to read a book that challenging. Whenever I read, it's more like Tom Clancy or Clive Cussler. "Couldn't finish? Or wouldn't?"

"Kind of the same? Neither up to the challenge, nor willing to try harder. Only so much time in the day," gesturing toward her bulging book bag. Becca, ready to get undergrad over and done with, had been taking eighteen hours that semester.

"A brainiac type like you?" Willing my eyes to twinkle. Winking at my lover, at our time together still dewy and new. "I thought you lived for that stuff."

"I do. But Casey, I'm only human. A girl needs other things." I felt her bare toes, wiggling and playful, on my shin. "Besides books and literary theories about them."

"I see."

I remember how the light from the beer signs glimmered kaleidoscopic on her glasses. "Yes. You will."

"I will?"

Nodding. "I'm going to show you."

That's what reminds me of her right now—I catch a flash of neon glinting off a shiny surface, and think that Becca's sitting there again.

Only she's not.

And won't be.

Thought I was over her, or at least getting her out of my system, until one day when I heard that David Foster Wallace had hung himself. I'd never own up to having done so now, but when I read the blurb about the suicide on CNN.com I burst into hot, hateful, hungry tears; for about an hour afterward I thought I was losing my mind. I didn't make the connection, not at first.

But I came into work, and saw the booth. The situation racked into focus like one of my disused, dusty camera lenses sitting on a high shelf way in the back of a closet.

Becca.

Writing her paper.

Infinite Jest.

Might as well have never happened.

She wanted to write her own books, Becca said; or failing that, edit other people's. Maybe eventually teach literary theory. All of it went well beyond either my experience or my ambition—I thought I'd be a photographer, but not in an artistic sense. More workmanlike. Portraits. Weddings. Paid gigs. It hasn't come together yet. I don't really pursue it.

Before she left, Becca let me read some of her short stories. I thought they were pretty good, kind of abstract. Sent me to the dictionary a couple of times a page. The bartender story, she warned, might sting. It didn't, only that her details about how it feels to work on the other side of the bar didn't feel real.

That's when I started collecting words, after reading her work. Trying to keep up. It ended up not mattering. All was fine, you see, until she decided to go to another school for her MFA. And when I offered to come with her, she declined.

BECCA HAD two big slobbery golden retrievers named Parsley and Sage, with frayed bandanas tied 'round their necks like in that sad Stephen Malkmus song about the mismatched couple who don't work out because of their differences in age and temperament. On Sundays we would take her pets to the dog park. The dog park, where I'll never go again even should I one day acquire my own. The park, the place where she told me that, as much as she liked me, she thought with grad school looming, and a move away from here imminent, well: that we should try calling it friendship, and go from there.

"I'll be back at the holidays. We'll get caught up then."

"Sure. We'll hang out."

"It's a plan."

After ruing the sensation of having ice water dumped over my head, I joked that grad school was for chumps. That she didn't need to move, not with so many jobs in the hospitality trade available, all positions, I noted, that lacked the requirement of a terminal postgraduate degree.

Together long enough, for heaven's sake, to have come up with a nickname of endearment: "Grad school, Becky-Bo? Who needs it."

She asked that I stop joking.

"I'm not. Not really."

A cloud of unease across her dimpled face. "I've had such a good time since the first of the year."

Ouch. "A good time. I get it."

"It's okay to be friends, isn't it? Like how this all started?"

I barked an aggrieved epithet, which prompted from her the two worst words in the whole cursed language:

"I'm sorry."

For the rest of the day, heartache bloomed inside me like metastasizing cancer, tumors of regret and yearning that grew for weeks afterwards.

Months.

Two years, now.

But only pangs. Occasional fleeting ouches in my gut where warmth once pulsed. Like, every night when I trudge into work and see the Booth Where She Studied.

BECCA, at six months, constituted my longest relationship since my other great love, Alice Faith, and that's all the way back when I was a fifth-year senior, dragging out the last couple of semesters and living pretty high off the loan checks. I had been working at the independent camera store, a mom and pop enterprise passed down to a son who sat watching the business get squeezed by the big boxes out on the beltway. That job didn't work out, but I did manage to get some cheap gear. And meet Alice Faith.

Another media major like me, she had been a sophomore taking the B&W Photography class I'd aced two years prior. I had noticed her and spoken in passing around the media hallways and classrooms. One afternoon she came into the camera store. I flirted like mad and tried to sounded knowledgeable, a photographic badass with scads of experience under my belt.

She made a camera purchase and we set up a casual date. Afterwards, we hung out for three or four fun-filled months. Much to the chagrin of rent-paying roommates inconvenienced by such behavior, we had noisy coitus and bounced around town on each other's arms like young couples tend to do.

About that time I started bar-backing at McHaffie's Pub to make some extra scratch. I had begun thinking about asking if she wanted to get a place together.

The day came. The camera store owner formally announced that his business struggled to compete with the big bad corporate outlets, and how he's sorry but everyone's hours were now to be cut. Worse, as low man I got cut altogether. Laid off.

I thought, well, it's no big deal. I have to finish school; I also now have McHaffie's. I had options, short term as well as long.

But soon after I got let go from the camera store, Alice Faith met this dude finishing up a master's in international business, and as fast as you can snap your fingers at a slow server, I found myself wrapping fish like yesterday's newsprint.

A semi-tearful breakup ensued. Alice Faith came off contrite but blunt, explaining that true love was what it was, and should only be ignored at risk of enormous emotional peril. Later that summer they got married. I heard they had a kid about seven-point-five months after the wedding night. I didn't, and do not, care.

Maybe sometimes. When I miss her pretty face. Which is usually only after I finish feeling sorry for myself about Becca.

~

AFTER ALICE FAITH dumped me I managed to finish my degree, got drunk for a week, and went full time at McHaffie's while I figured out what to do next on the road of life.

Worked for three months like a crazed monkey stacking bananas. I saw no shame in tending bar to make do until a break came my way, one sure to happen to someone like me, who maybe didn't so much deserve a break as feel that the odds of impending good fortune loomed favorable: law of averages, all that shit.

One day I decided on a whim to pack it in and go to Europe. Europe, I thought. I'll go to a faraway land, get my shit figured out. Meet the right lady along way. Who knew. Bought a Eurail pass. Bought a 40 liter backpack and a pair of Merrills.

I went into work to give notice. The owner of McHaffie's, Jay —or Jayboy, as everyone called him—looked at me with his cheeks sagging. I thought he was pissed, but instead he said, "By all means, go. If we can't squeeze you back in here after you get back, there's always another bar to work in somewhere —trust me."

"Don't want to leave you in the lurch."

"Dude—go to Europe. You have the rest of your life to work in a dump like this."

I took his advice: Amsterdam, Paris, Italy, Greece. Hostels, trains; hiking, hunger, hangovers. Taking hundreds of snaps, at least until my camera disappeared on me one night while camping with these cats in Greece, olive-skinned guys who spoke my language with reasonable fluency and who laughed a lot, seemed fun. Had a couple of girls show up; a real good time. We were drinking ouzo in a park and I got about as saturated as I've ever been, head spinning, finally passing out on a picnic table. Because they spoke English so well I had let my guard down, trusted those dudes.

Woke up to no camera or money. My folks had to wire me enough to make it back.

Heading back toward Amsterdam to fly home I met a French girl, Alexandra, who had been charmed by the American claiming to be a photographer and yet having no camera. A likely story. The best memories of the whole trip ended up being Alexandra's dark eyes flashing, the squeaking of the bed in a cheap room, her soft moans, the scent of her body earthy, spicy, unfamiliar; and the goodbye, at the train station.

A lingering hug. "I will see you again someday, I am certain," in her charming accent. "So long, Ca-zee. Not goodbye."

"So long. That sounds better."

I spent the rest of the trip in the Amsterdam coffee shops, got ripped on Afghani hash and tried to forget about the idea of ever seeing her again. Or Alice Faith, for that matter. I suffered the stuff of romantic, wistful remorse. Not so much for the acts them-selves, or their small number, only, I think, that I never got to know Alexandra any better than I did. Or Alice Faith.

Or Becca.

Or maybe it's that they get to know me too fast.

Ouch. Am I that bad?

"I THINK I'm in love with you."

I say this as Kaylee and I bump elbows, both trying to muddle mojitos from the same plastic sack of fresh mint leaves. Mojitos— jesus, what a bullshit rigmarole build, a drink that Paddy, a crusty old guy who savors single malt scotch and hates PC culture, calls 'faggoty': takes a long time to make, the customer drinks the damn thing down in half the time it takes to make it, and then? *They want another.*

Kaylee, cynical at my declaration of affection: "Oh, please."

"Maybe I'm serious."

She warns me not to joke about such matters of the heart, not to a girl between meaningfuls, as she terms relationships lasting longer than a weekend.

"I'd never lie to you."

"Gimme a break, Case Logic," a nickname she gave me one

day when I was flipping through an old binder of CDs. "I'm fragile right now."

Kaylee, a drama queen. Heard her call herself fragile more times than I can count.

Here's the thing. I feel like I know Kaylee. Wouldn't be like another drunken meaningless lay, bada bing and all that. We're already friends. A shorthand between us. Intimacy, of a kind.

"You're the most beautiful woman I know."

"Just make both of these fucking things, okay? I'll pull your ales for you."

"Beautiful, and giving. A rare combo. A sexy one."

A scoff and a frown—a curious one.

I make a perfect pair of mojitos; I'm a damn good bartender. Would that my pouring skills translated into matters of the heart. I present the drinks and the customers, a male-female version of the Blues Brothers, go ahead and order two more mojitos before they've even had a sip.

Now that it's ten Scottie's come on deck, which gives me the chance to accost Kaylee, whom I find removing her kittycat ears out on the back porch.

Her mascara, smudged from sweating during the shift, or else crying over Reedy's accusations. She looks cuddly in her South-eastern Redtails sweatshirt.

I grope and tickle ribs layered by cloth and flesh. Kiss her cheek.

"Um—sexual harassment, anyone?"

I pull her close. "So look: maybe I wasn't kidding."

"Casey."

"Yes?"

"I told you not to mess with me like that."

I take her face in my hands, which I made sure to wash before following her outside. "What are you doing tomorrow afternoon?"

She remains confused and wary. "What is this foolishness?"

"Totally serious."

"You want to take me out on a date?"

I do indeed; I tell her so. "I've liked you for a long-ass time."

"You have?"

"What's not to like?"

A cautious smile. "Why don't you call me tomorrow. We can talk then—just weird sometimes when you work with someone? To hook up? Don't you think?"

"I don't know. Let's figure it out."

"All right, honey." She gives me a sisterly peck on the cheek, goes back inside. "We'll get coffee. Like friends."

This is going nowhere. I feel like an idiot. Why Kaylee? Why now? Why not.

CRAPPY HOUR'S UPON US. A wave comes through the front door, goblins and witches and cheerleaders and fake rock stars with plastic guitars, whooping and hollering and ready to drink—it's the floor staff from the fern bar across from the fountain. Scottie has managed to get stoned enough to be a decent bartender for a change. We're all set.

A new round of pouring beers, making shots, straining to talk over the revelry. "I see they made y'all dress up," I yell to Carla, a cute hostess from the restaurant who appears tonight as a Johnny Depp-style pirate. "How were tips?"

A sour face. Slurring: "Like, for shit."

Fewer tips means less to tip me. Wait, what am I saying? These folks work in the trade. They'll tip out.

"Casey—will you do a shot with us?"

"Sure."

I make the shots, a stupid sweet one called a Purple Hooter. After I do one, the group clustered at the elbow of the bar cheers, but I feel a cold hole open in the middle of my body, like the liquor has burned straight through.

More off-the-clock bartenders come in. I turn down another shot, make a chocolatini or two, make a bourbon rocks with a water back, pull pints, make G&Ts. I keep looking for Becca, have to remind myself that I'll settle for my friends Mel and Johnna, loyal early morning cowgirls who'll close down the biker bar on the other side of the Market and amble over here in time to greet the sunrise and start relaxing. Far from Halloween ghosts, these women present instead as real and tangible. But only friends.

Thinking of Johnna makes me reconsider asking Kaylee out. Johnna, a bartender for 15 years now, has wisdom. She's always talking about the do's and don'ts of working in the trade. For instance, never to fuck your coworkers or your boss.

Oops. Maybe she's wrong about that.

Another bit of wisdom, this one offered at about ten *ayeem* one morning while we sat getting drunk as hell watching the *Today* show together, the bile from doing shots of Maker's lapping at the back of my throat, briny and acidic as a polluted harbor.

Johnna, besotted yet lucid, explained: "You can party alongside your customers, sure, but you've got to stay one stair-step less fucked up than them."

"Because—?"

"Because that's when you get ripped off."

"You mean people skipping out on tabs?"

"Well, there's that. But it's that you stop caring about the quality of your service. Which is what gets you the choice tips. Which is where the real money is."

I understood completely, told her so. Johnna, a pro.

FOR SOME REASON, though, Mel and Johnna don't show up on this waning Halloween night, and people stagger out earlier than normal; by six-thirty—the Day of the Dead—we're winding it down and buttoning her up.

What do you know—Scottie and I get done in time to see the first lilac band of sunrise appear over tops of the downtown buildings.

"So I heard a rumor." Outside on the street, Scottie, pulling his jacket tight against the chill of the first of November. "You hear it, too?"

I remember Reedy, and his visit last night. "Someone's getting fired."

"Not exactly."

"What, then? Closing the place?"

"All-but: I heard Reedy wants to sell this dump."

Terrible news. "A new boss? That's just what we need."

"Heard he wants to sell, but to someone who loves the place like he does."

I absorb this remark. "Really, now."

"S'what I heard. Take it easy."

"Take it sleazy."

Scottie gets into his shitbox Jetta and drives off, leaving me alone but for the dawn and the songbirds and the garbage trucks rumbling along.

Maybe I'll talk to Reedy. Couldn't hurt. Reedy, he gets his rest, has a good life, a family, a good wife. He got there somehow.

Not somehow—he took a first step, as he always says, by becoming a small business owner.

By owning this dump.

HELL, I like this job, even if it's temporary until I get my shit together. The money's good; hours weird, but that can be fixed. The normal everyday world turns on a different axis from mine, people living their lives exposed and examined beneath the harsh scrutiny of the noonday sun. Meanwhile, I'm hiding safe beneath the cloak of darkness—a nocturnal wraith taking the pulse of the nightswept city, waiting for sleepless drinkers to come in, for folks to order and consume, for customers to offer remuneration for a service most valuable: the transfer of spirits from one vessel to another. It is thus that the vampire shift—the wages of SIN—sustains me.

For now. Besides, if Scottie's full of beans about Reedy's intentions? I have options. Two words: grad school. Maybe at the college where Becca's teaching. Wherever that is. I'll think about it. Get some sleep. I have the night off later. I think I could use it.

AUTHOR NOTE: ORIGINALLY ENTITLED 'VAMPIRE SHIFT,' I sent this story out quite a few times before reading a do's and don't's blog post about submitting short stories, and a big no-no, as it turns out, is the collegiate neighborhood bartender story. Oops. Guess quite a few English majors are out there slinging liquor to make ends meet. This one's for all of you. Unpublished, except as a post at my blog, Edgewater County Confidential.

LOCKED IN THE PUNCH

Central Park, greener and more alive than it had a right to be in the middle of a stony hive like Manhattan, stretched into the distance from the hotel room window of Dr. Kip Epperton, DVM. As an anticipatory vibration snaked along his spinal column, Dr. Kip stood awash in confidence and certitude, ate a snack-pack chocolate pudding, and grinned at the thought of the mission that lay ahead.

His true motivations for the trip, hidden from his family and peers.

And yet they knew. Had to. Would be fools to not get it by now.

Forget the veterinary conference—a subterfuge. An excuse. No more plenary sessions and panels and hobnobbing with the other vets at the professional gathering, no; no more sales pitches from the pharma reps.

No.

Kip, in possession of other plans.

To wit: With lilac dawn breaking across the skyline of this towering pinnacle of a city so far from his Southern, small town home, Kip basked in the esoteric knowledge that Kaufman Day

2014—a day of magic—had arrived. As had Kip, a man fully formed amidst the fecund flowering of springtime resplendence.

Apt, he thought. *I flower anew.*

Kip had come to the veterinary conference in New York for one reason, the fortuitous coincidence of the professional gathering occurring the same week as the long-held red letter day, 16 May 2014. The decision to blow off that morning's workshop on advances in feline leukemia treatment, as well as all other official functions, had been a fait accompli funded by the well-heeled clientele of Sunnyvale Animal Clinic back home in South Carolina. He served them well; it was but turnabout fair-play that he now be served.

Kip, singing an interior song like a mantra—*thirty years, thirty years.* Not so long, not in the grand scheme of things. A blip. A chunk, granted, of a man's life, but to the cosmos? An infinitesimal microsecond.

A blip-chunk.

Which brought up a nagging question: Kip wondered how the interval had passed for Andy.

A long slog?

Or the blink of an eye?

His own experience? A 35 year-old veterinary physician strolling through the great city to a subway that'd take him to the station where he'd catch the **LIRR** train, swearing to himself how only a split second before he'd been 15, watching the tribute to Andy on cable TV, and having his mind expanded. Absorbing the high praise from other entertainers who held the man, 'dead' only a decade, in such godlike esteem.

All roads lead to Andy, one of them had said with reverence, a TV comedian skilled in the art of mimicry.

He knew the man spoke of the art of comedy, but for Kip the words were felt and understood on a more personal level. Kaufman existed above and beyond the norm. This became clear to Kip in an instant indelible and life-changing. Like old people recalled their whereabouts during various assassinations or moon landings or celebrity criminal trial verdicts, for Kip, it had been the Andy Kaufman Tribute television special. Everyone's path to enlightenment was different.

"THE RESURRECTION IS NIGH."

Kip said this to a religious pamphleteer, a squat, gray-faced man built like a fire hydrant and distributing tracts on a platform inside Penn Station, an eddy amidst a roiling, cacophonous white-water of humanity going every which way.

A woolen overcoat despite the mild air, with a strange, unfamiliar accent—nothing like Foreign Man, however—the zealot's eyes shone, but far from affected, more like sincere. "The savior, he is soon to come."

Kip smirked and winked. "True enough; but wrong water-walker, my friend."

"Oh—there is another savior?" The man shook his head at Kip. His words sounded ponderous and sad. "This, it is wonderful news. But highly unlikely."

Kip, feeling played. "Wise guy."

Swigging a mango peach-flavored Diet Snapple, he moved down the platform to wait for the train. Kip, certain Andy's reappearance would indeed serve as a prophecy, if not a spiritual actualization of enormous cosmic magnitude; and all on the cusp of fulfillment and fruition. If that wasn't good news, he'd like to know what was.

But Andy would not arise from the cesspool known as Hollywood as in his prior incarnation, no. Rather, the miracle to occur in a place as ordinary and American as Great Neck—Elmont, actually—where the Beth David cemetery was located. But taking the train to Great Neck, to first visit Andy's childhood home, on the off chance that something might happen there. Innocence and wonder and play, all had been inherent to childhood, as well as Andy Kaufman's act.

And, who better to make this pilgrimage?

After all, Kip administered the foremost net wiki about Andy Kaufman, stood tall in the saddle as expert and master, so much that he felt a kinship with his subject going well beyond typical fandom: Andy to Kip was like Garcia to a Deadhead—the fount. The reason for the season. The secret. The glue that held the grand design together; the reality that wasn't reality, but beyond the ordinary plane of existence most people knew and understood. Andy represented the possibility that all was not what it seemed.

But as Kip often said, "Those who don't know don't know they don't know, and those who do? Well, they ain't telling." Kip, happy to truth-tell to anyone who'd listen.

In a troubling development, however, few with whom he crossed paths seemed interested. Their loss, thought Kip.

Andy himself had written a play, one 'posthumously' published by his family, called *God*. Kip Epperton thought this an apropos title; he indeed believed that God, whatever It was, worked through Andy, and as a result, through Kip. Whispering. A message. Something like, who you people gonna believe—me, or your lying eyes?

Andy's own words, from the text of *God*:

Hearken thou: Art sinners all. I see ye in thou bloomers everyday picking bits from one another's brows. Thou art comely into forbidden grounds.

THOU SHALT SUFFER, my friend . . .

But for Kip, the suffering soon to end.

His logic, infallible: If Andy were to reappear—*if* meaning *when*—the symmetry offered by reappearing at his own supposed site of internment had to hold strong appeal. To roll out the punchline to the grandiloquent and marvelous prank that Kaufman had perpetuated, could there be a more apt locale? Discerning this eventuality had been another important *ah-ha* moment for Kip, coming to him during a particularly routine procedure to remove a dog's testicles.

As he stood on the steel and concrete platform that vibrated at various levels of intensity and suffered physical jostling by the multitudes awaiting the train, a moment of faith-shaking doubt gurgled along his GI tract like bloating flatus. After all this time, and after all the disappointments, did Kip still believe enough in the dream? That what lay as moldy myth to others would for him become tangible reality?

Yes. This belief, in a sense, represented all that he possessed.

"You told us you'd return." Kip said this to no one as the LIRR trundled and rocked along its tracks into the station, and the throng moved as one toward the demarcated boarding areas. "And being a man of character, Andy, so you shall."

Kip, the train bearing him toward an Omega point of personal destiny and feeling as though he floated lighter than the helium in a child's party balloon, sat in repose, staring straight ahead; not reading, not thinking, in a kind of fugue state like meditation; and if it wasn't quite TM, he remained sure Andy would be proud of the discipline, Kip's meticulous control of mind, body, and spirit. Getting in the right headspace to greet the master upon his return from the void, why, anything less would serve to disrespect all Andy had sought to achieve.

Anything less?

The efforts of a loser.

And Kip, like Andy, presented as no loser. Not on the outside, anyway.

THE CAB RIDE from the Long Island train platform in the light midmorning traffic only took a few minutes. First stop, the unassuming childhood home in Great Neck, whereupon seeing no discernible spiritual activity, Kip bade the driver to depart with all speed for Elmont.

The cemetery. Where all the action would happen.

Kip, buzzing and bouncing on the seat like a child being taken to the circus, engaged the cabbie, a young, beautifully complexioned African man whose hack license read that he was Mamadou Blé from the Republic of Côte d'Ivoire.

"Sir—a question. You have TV back home?"

"TV? Yah, yah. Course." Frowning in the rearview. "Duddent everyone, hey?"

"Indeed. Ever see a sitcom called *Taxi*?"

"Sit-com? What you mean?"

"A show. A TV show with jokes—you know, comedy." Well, on the show Andy'd been more than a mere comic foil, of course, but this, a finely pointed detail best left out of the conversation at hand. "You know. Like *Seinfeld*, or *Two and a Half Men*."

"Oh, ha-ha, yah. Charlie Sheen, he winning. But, *Taxi*—like in, taxi cab?" He nodded, seemed quite amused. "I get it. I get it, hey."

"That's correct. It's one of the most important shows ever."

"I got to see dat one? Yeah?"

"By all means. Today, if possible."

"What the rush?"

Kip, glowing with foreknowledge like a fever inside. "You'll find out."

He gulped air and began to lay out the whole bit about why *Taxi* was truly important—how its largesse had financed and made possible Andy's stardom and freedom to pursue his performance art—and why Dr. Kip Epperton sat cabbing around Long Island and what the day meant and what was likely to happen; in other words, nothing short of an earthshaking event in the course of human history masquerading as the culmination of the greatest prank of the mass media and information age. This day would herald the start of a new epoch in performance art, elevating what had heretofore been easy to dismiss as mere standup comedy now taken a degree, or perhaps a thousand-million degrees, farther than the norm of telling jokes and expecting laughs, which Andy had of course achieved in 'life' already.

But a little voice had warned: *Don't say any of that because the dude ain't gonna get it. You can't lay truth on them all at once like that.*

Story of a life. With whom had Kip been able to share this knowledge?

No one; and no-thing.

Alas, ruminating piteous upon his mateless existence here on the high holiday of 16 May wouldn't solve any cosmic conundrums. Through the years he'd gone out on dates, yes, but once he'd started in on his various obsessions, his companions invariably seemed nonplussed to find out the handsome vet was not only a geek, but an Andy geek at that.

He had recently tried again with a woman. Determined to keep quiet about Andy, Kip had taken out a beautiful local musician named Marcy Baumbach, but every conversation feint he attempted led back to Andy; and by the end of the evening, the woman's normally healthy and glowing countenance had turned sallow and wan. Far from succeeding, that night Kip suffered a particularly unbridled incidence of Andy logorrhea. It had happened only because he'd liked Marcy; he'd really, really liked her. Getting-to-know-you had gotten out of hand.

Women. He wrestled with figuring them out.

The cab arrived at the gate of Beth David. Mamadou glanced at the cemetery, put a hand over his heart. "I'm sorry, hey, for your loss."

Kip, reduced by the sentiment to giggles which he was certain the cabbie took for sobbing. "Yeah, sure. Thanks."

"You wanna me to wait?"

"No. I'm not sure how long I'll be."

Kip tipped Mamadou the cabbie and reached to shake his hand. Instead, the hack pressed together hands in a prayerful *namaste* before motoring away in a little puff of blue-gray exhaust.

"*Taxi*," Kip called after the taxi. "Check it out."

Watching the cab disappear, he wiped tears from his eyes, happy, Andy-worthy joyful weeping. But then, Kip, head on a swivel, felt a bloom of half-disappointment that this place, too, seemed deserted.

~

KIP WAITED near the Kaufman plot. He sat staring at the small, unassuming slab of marble imbedded in the ground—a shrine sacred yet profane, as he thought of the marker. Sunlight shafted through the trees. Spidery shadows cast by leafy windblown limbs danced across Andy Kaufman's tombstone with the rhythm of a chuckle. Birds sang a happy *tweet-tweet* morning tune.

Kip, wavering, prayed for a sign. He knelt and danced trembling fingertips across the tombstone, touching the raised lettering. The Jewish writing held no meaning for him.

How Andy must have snickered when he'd discussed with his family what to put on the stone; how generic the marker seemed. Andy, so much more than a beloved son, brother, grandson; his own family knowing this, of course, but in on the gag.

Kip had so much respect for the Kaufman family, the ones who had also needed to exercise considerable discipline and courage and patience across the expanse of time that had elapsed since 1984. He had hoped to meet them one of these years.

A bright yellow butterfly fluttered in his field of vision, and he exulted at the inherent positivity.

Across the cemetery, he watched through narrowed lids as an actual funeral took place—a knot of black and gray stick figures, the cluster of colorful flowers, a man in black reading from a book. He could detect murmuring on the wind.

"Ashes to ashes," Kip said. "Back to the dust."

A rare and immersive peace came over Dr. Kip Epperton: Andy staged a funeral not unlike that real one, in the very spot where Kip stood with his back against a mature hardwood tree. Chicken-skin broke out along his skinny arms.

He'd always been too thin, never able to gain an ounce. He ate cheeseburgers, of which Andy wouldn't have approved, and lots of chocolate cake, which Andy would have endorsed, but Kip still weighed the same as he had at 15. The age of First Contact with Andy's world. Manhood, in his case, heralded in the form of the Andy tribute, a kind of secularly comedic bar mitzvah.

He addressed the marker. "You laid it all out for us, didn't you?"

The tombstone, mute, implacable, stared back.

Kip, undeterred, rubbed his hands together. "You said—and these are your words, Andy—that if you were going to do it, to make it truly worth everyone's while? To make the event your return needed to be, to have the significance, the impact, one going beyond some mere show business publicity stunt? You said you'd wait a long time. Twenty years: that's what you told Lynn."

Kip's voice broke. "Well, in oh-four we found out that twenty wasn't enough. Same deal in 2009—twenty-five, not enough. Andy, I get it. Thirty—that's a number people can get their heads around."

No reply beyond more chittering, chattering birdsong.

"*I said*," he called out, "*I get it, Andy*."

Elation. Fresh certitude—an assurance beyond reason— flooded into Kip's body like cold adrenaline. Without warning he kicked out his elbows and launched into a spastic, freaky head-whipping dance; he mimed the playing of congas. Then, as quickly as the urge had come over him, it left. Sometimes Andy seemed to pass through Kip like a restless, peripatetic spirit borne upon invisible breezes.

"I figured you out," thrusting an accusatory finger at Andy's grave. "Busted. Thirty it is, then. See you in a bit."

INDEED, said twenty-year mark had come and gone with Kip standing on much the same spot, breathless, waiting and watching the clock turn over to midnight. But the moment, as well as the whole day, had yielded no known appearance by Andy.

Between Kaufman Day 2004 and 2009, Kip became degreed and plunged headlong into his career working with the other vets over at the bustling practice in a Sedge Island, South Carolina low-country suburb of bourgeois Southern folks. Some of them came in acting as though the animals were their precious beloved children, while others behaved as though the creatures were but another possession—like a broken toaster in need of repair, or their fine automobile whose onboard computer had called for routine servicing. Kip treated the latter clients with professionalism and attention to detail—it was no less than any sick animal deserved—but the owners themselves received only a clinician's icy disdain. Kip could slip in and out of character as easily as changing into a fresh pair of socks and wrestling tights.

Like someone else he knew.

Someone special.

Someone watching over him.

Over time Kip acquired a sense of unbridled optimism that led him along a familiarly speculative path—the notion that Andy had possibly come back on any or all prior occasions, but he'd chosen to remain silent simply to add an even more abstruse element to the overall tapestry of pseudo- and hyper-reality surrounding the life and mind of the 'late' comedian.

One school of thought held that Andy had never really left. Rather, he had had extensive plastic surgery and lived far from the spotlight he'd once ostensibly craved, working as an ordinary man at an ordinary trade in a typical town. At times, every Caucasian middle-aged man of medium build and dark curly hair who crossed his path caught Kip's eye, goosed his adrenal glands, fired his imagination.

Andy could be anywhere, Kip realized one day. *He could be everywhere.*

BEFORE KIP'S ascension to full consciousness circa 1995, Andy had been opaque. Born in 1979, young Epperton possessed neither memories of seeing his idol on first run episodes of *Taxi*

nor the artist's landmark appearances on *SNL*, the *Fridays* incident, the wrestling, the talk show appearances. None of Andy's other work, not in a firsthand primary-source sense.

With revelatory and epiphanic precision, the nature of Kaufman's genius—his gift to the world—had been ratcheted into sharp focus for Kip by the tribute special. Before, he'd only thought he admired the comedians and actors praising Andy. But after discovering Andy Kaufman, the rest presented as rank and mediocre philistines, their only saving grace an apparent grasp that, however talented or successful or wealthy, when compared to Andy, they presented as pretenders to the legitimate throne.

Hell—they all knew it. Seemed in mild embarrassment at finding themselves on camera in the presence of the clips.

The last piece of the puzzle had been Kip's discovery regarding Andy's fixation with faking his death. About staying away so long that people would give up.

Would even forget about him, perhaps.

And then—only then—to return.

Next stop, Goosebump City.

A HUSHED FEMALE VOICE, lilting from behind him. "Excuse me—?"

Kip, heart pounding in throat, whirled around to see a youngish, frizzy-haired bespectacled woman wearing Birkenstocks, jeans, and a Tony Clifton T-shirt.

"Oh." Her face, crestfallen. "Oh, god."

"You startled the freaking mess out of me."

"I'm so sorry."

Kip scrutinized her. "Here for a funeral?"

"Not exactly." The woman carried a bouquet of fresh flowers, vivid coloration like a swath of rainbow she'd captured and clutched close to her ample bosom. Sheepish. "I brought these. For Andy."

Kip bloomed with warmth. "Well, bless your heart."

"Thing is, I thought—for a minute—that—that you—"
Downcast eyes. "Well. As if."

Kip stood aside. "That's terribly sweet. But, no."

She placed the flowers on the earth.

He smiled—she was in on the gag. "They're beautiful."

"It's the least I could do on the sixteenth of May."

Kip, silent and awkward. An Eastern towhee went *vreet vreet*.
"Too bad he's not here to see this lovely display."

"Too bad."

Gathering his wits, Kip asked the woman, who introduced
herself as Sheba MacElhaney, if she wished to join him in waiting.
She did.

A FADING HANDWRITTEN notice tacked to the bulletin board in the
vet office waiting room. Yellowed, the corners starting to curl up,
it read in Comic Sans typeface:

Dr. Kip Wants Your
TOYS, GAMES, MOVIE POSTERS
and Other
POP CULTURE EPHEMERA
from the 60s, 70s and 80s.
Inquire at staff desk.

NO NEED FOR ANDY STUFF, of course, but Kip, a man of many
tastes and proclivities, obsessively collected crucial artifacts of the
modern, civilized communication and entertainment age. Totems
and fetishes; pieces of history held in trembling, appreciative,
white-gloved hands. Kip, an archivist, a curator, an historian with

a veritable warehouse of material, doing the future a favor. The largest storage shed available in a climate controlled facility near his condo sat lined with expensive top-drawer metal shelving, all items organized, catalogued, neat and clean.

For Kip, the relics left behind—like Andy himself—had always been about a transcendence of ordinary time and space, an assurance of immortality, the through-line, the thread. The icons of pop culture—Western twentieth century pop culture, and Kip didn't mean Western as in *Gunsmoke* or *The Virginian*, Western, like, you know, English-speaking books and movies and TV type stuff—lived on, in fact thrived. Chaplin, Marilyn, James Dean, the Three Stooges, Groucho Marx, Hitchcock, Elvis, John Lennon, Kurt Cobain, Michael Jackson: surviving, influencing, their personas like living, breathing, sentient creatures capable of action and motion and visceral emotional impact well beyond the hazy blue veil of death.

Andy, knowing this, and understanding such power.

Andy, evermore.

But, oh, with Andy, so much more! Creating that enduring indelible yet impossible to define persona—no mean feat—but in his case *remaining alive to control his memory from beyond the grave.*

Kip, shuddering at the recognition of genius, of spiritual and intellectual mastery.

A collector from childhood, from action figures to comics to movie crap and back to action figures, Kip, able to remember a time before the pervasive penetration of home video devices, when owning a movie or TV show was only as possible as personal memory allowed, or otherwise only in the form of ancillary artifacts: soundtracks, publicity stills, merchandising tie-ins, magazines, novelizations, comic adaptations, posters, press books, lobby cards, toys, games.

Kip's movie poster collection remained close to his heart, but insured and stored as it was in a huge flattened stack of acid-free cardboard sheets in a corner of the warehouse, and of late rarely accessed, the key art of countless movies sat dusty and untouched. Not forgotten; like all his objects, thoughts of the posters offered a comforting sensation of longevity and continuity.

The last one-sheet Kip actively collected? The big budget Hollywood-style Andy biopic, of course. A no-brainer.

~

"The cow goes moo," Kip said. "The birds go tweet-tweet." Sheba sighed. They watched as the cemetery workers used a small backhoe to complete the burial from the earlier funeral.

When they didn't talk, Sheba and Kip still seemed to be talking. He thought it was weird. But cool, too.

The hours passed in Beth David, and still no Andy.

Not yet.

Andy or no Andy, Kip and Sheba, as it turned out, fit together like hand in glove:

"To me," Sheba MacElhaney stated as though cribbing notes from a tome called *The Philosophy of Kip Epperton*, "Andy represented life and light and love; pop culture elevated to the level of the mystic and the metaphysical. A transmutation of spirit."

"He knew something the rest of us didn't."

"And still don't."

"For now."

Sheba, a flicker of sheepish doubt. "Do you really think he'll return?"

"Would I be here otherwise?" Kip, feeling like an elder, a magus, to this woman. "From blindness to sight."

"Yes." Sheba, her mouth a downturned half-circle. "Not today, though."

A deep breath; a grim admission. "Patience is required by the penitent. May they find it bequeathed unto them."

"What if it's more than patience?"

"Explain."

"Maybe it's a puzzle."

Kip, nodding. Getting a little of his old spark back. "Maybe outside Carnegie Hall? In time to make the evening newscast?"

Sheba, nodding. "We could still make the last train into the city."

With only the smallest of catches in his voice: "Maybe in the end it's neither here nor there."

"Like, literally."

Along with the lengthening of the shadows and the changing of the light, the birds had quieted. "I can't believe how long we've been out here. The day flew by."

"I enjoyed myself," Sheba said.

Kip stood and stretched, cracking his back. "You must have taken off work."

Sheba seemed embarrassed. "I own a comics and collectibles shop. I closed it to come here today."

Kip stirred as one's soul does at hearing a favorite TV show theme, watching the opening crawl of a *Star Wars* movie—the original trilogy, not the prequels—or like the triumphant day the VHS of Andy's famous Carnegie Hall special had arrived in the mail. How Kip trembled as the videocassette had loaded into the player. How he had felt a bloom of fire in his gut, like the time as a child when he'd accidentally taken a drink of wine he'd thought grape juice: revelatory, almost painful.

Unforgettable.

Like Sheba's face.

He didn't know who Sheba was, or what she represented—not yet—but perhaps for the first time in his life, Kip Epperton at last knew himself. Or rather, knew he wasn't alone in the universe. He'd always hoped that, so long as Andy was still out there some-where—always and forever; the nothing within the everything; the one without a two—there could be no true solitude. Only now Kip had found someone with whom to share his own secret knowledge, his sense of self, of purpose, and the wholeness and oneness of life.

A life shared.

A life that's real.

Real as real ever seems, anyway.

Kip brushed grass and twigs from the seat of his khakis; Sheba did the same from her faded denims, then squatted and retied her black Chuck Taylors, stood, squatted, and repeated the sequence. "I'm a little OCD."

"I have to lock the door three times when I leave the house."

They hugged, spontaneous.

Kip pushed back. "I need to ask you something."

Sheba smiled. "I hope you don't want me to touch a cyst on your neck."

"Not even for a dollar?"

Shaking her head.

"Not even for free?"

"Nope."

Kip, warmed by the obscure Andy reference. He counted this as another among a growing surfeit of Sheba's bonafides. Assured in his belief this represented only the beginning of all Sheba would say to him, he found the courage and formed the words: "If we could, I'd rather skip Carnegie Hall."

"I'm shocked."

"Instead, I'd like to go and see your memorabilia."

"Is that a come-on?"

"It's not meant to be blue material." Kip, a gentleman, offered reassurance. "I promise."

Sheba, taking him by the hand and leading him toward the gate. "Some promises are meant to be broken. That's the point of them." As they made their way from the Andy gravesite, they did so hand in hand and never more than a millimeter apart.

A middle-aged man with pasty skin, a paunch and an Elvis pompadour sat on the bus stop bench. He peered over a newspaper and tipped an imaginary hat, but Kip, hardly noticing. Not now that he had Sheba by his side.

∾

AUTHOR NOTE: A finalist for both the Faulkner-Wisdom Award (2012) and Red Hen Press/LA Weekly Fiction Award (2013), many prior versions of this tribute to a personal pop culture icon, Andy Kaufman, made the rounds without finding a home. This latest version, refined a touch from the prior submission version that did so well, may not seem like it at first, but fits into the Edgewater County mythos when protagonist Dr. Kip makes a key cameo appearance in the upcoming novel Down in Dixiana.

HOWDY FROM UPSTAIRS

Captain Mandrake, as he calls himself, strides into the room —a living space, warm, cluttered, three generations' worth of portraiture and bric-a-brac, the only sound the crackling of a dying fire—and proceeds, as he is wont to do, to cause me no shortage of distress: It is late, and the chill of January has settled over the world. I am reading; I am at a good part. It is my one escape, this.

But by now, I am used to the routine. I'm just especially tired tonight.

"Go ahead," I say to him. I look down; my toenails appear dry. I start pulling out the little foam dividers. "What is tonight's grand revelation?"

He shoots me a withering look, then paces back and forth, his hands jammed into the pockets of our grandmother's robe. She doesn't need it anymore. "Ever so impatient," he says, scratching his stubble. I don't think he's changed his shirt for a month, now —I think he just keeps Febreze'ing it every few days. The front of it looks like a Pollack interpretation of my brother's last couple of dozen meals.

"Yes, but—"

"That book's eating you alive, that fiction. Take a breather, General Ripper."

I look down at the volume, a collection of thrilling and implausible stories. Engrossing, unchallenging, chock full of incident; forward narrative momentum that pauses neither for breath nor logic. Gunplay. Betrayal. Intimations of erotic congress, though not explicit. Fade-outs as in tame movies; a diffusion and then black as the bedroom door closes and our imaginations fill the empty spaces with our interpretation of that which the lovers do to one another. (*With* one another, I mean.) I teach the real stories all day long, "A Rose for Emily" and "Good Country People"; the bad stuff helps me relax. Turns off the brain. Lets me be someone else for a while. My secret shame.

I don't know that I can take the routine tonight. *"Howdy,"* I plead.

"Tut-tut." He turns on me, wagging a finger.

He hates that nickname—Howdy—but too bad, to me that's who he'll always be. I gave it to him when we were kids because Howard sounds so stuffy, antiquated, even. Howdy is more than a name, it's a cheerful greeting. But in the end the Chamberlain in me chooses appeasement, rapprochement, even: "All right, Group Captain Lionel Mandrake. Better?"

"I should say so," in a clipped, reasonable Peter Sellers. The Captain Mandrake Peter Sellers, that is. "Yes, yes. May I proceed with my report, General?"

I close my book. I sigh and sink back into the easy chair; I gesture in a helpless expression of *what other choice do I have?*

"Very well, then."

It's cold in the room. I swing my feet over in front of the embers. I ought to throw on another shank of cordwood, but I'd have to go all the way out back. Even colder out there. Dark, out in the country. Besides, it's Howdy's job to bring the wood inside.

Mandrake—my brother, older than me, back home from the wars, as he tells it—proceeds to regale me with the protracted preamble to his main point, which is always the same point, only with modest variations. The oration rambles on—childhood minutiae, a missing pet, a locker room embarrassment, a failed college romance, a marriage, a divorce…

But also nice things, here and there: a magical sunset on a Boy Scout camping trip, a ball game in the bright sunshine with an old childhood friend, a walk alongside a field of sunflowers in resplendent full bloom (a new bit—a fabrication?). Various and sundry triumphs, tragedies, impressions, life lessons.

My eyes droop.

"But then I truly lost everything." This is the jumping off point from his near-boilerplate prologue, that which is altered and revised only just so in the telling each night. Now to the main event of the evening, the feature presentation:

The plans for the future. These plans are the meat, the entrée, the main course. These plans, these are what keep the audience interested—these are the surprises, the plot twists, the new material that he's trying out like a fourth-rate comic working the chitlin circuit before hitting the big towns, refining the material, writing new jokes, creating a theme for the act. That the plans are always words and not eventual deeds does not seem to factor into the telling, this nocturnal ritual. I think he does it to let me know that he's all right, that he's not completely lost in the wilderness of his illness. That he's looking ahead to some positive goal, like any normal person would.

"And the conclusion I've now come to, sir?

"Yes, oh Captain, my Captain?"

"Sales. *Sales.* I have always been a salesman at heart."

"*Yes?*"

"Think about it."

"I'm trying." I squeeze my eyes shut, pretending to concentrate. "Okay, I thought about it."

"Good. Now: Fuller brushes, vacuum cleaners. Magazine subscriptions. Newspaper subscriptions. Digital satellite television subscriptions. Homeopathic health care remedies. Cosmetics, even—gender specific roles are passé. Encyclopedias. Insurance policies—peace of mind, in other words, and that's something they say you can't buy." He's wound up now. "Investment opportunities—no, scratch that. Let's see: Automobiles. Real estate. Foodstuffs. Wholesale goods and services. Cardboard boxes. Styrofoam peanuts. Plastic food wrap. Astringents. Emulsifiers. Manufactured housing. Precious metal futures. Oil futures. Porkbelly futures…! Gah." He turns white as a bleached sheet. "*Scratch* that, I say."

"But, that *is* something you know all about…"

He stands there in the middle of the rug with his hands on his hips and looks up to the ceiling. I can hear his neck pop. "Ah. *Ah.* But here it is, what I was leading up to: The sale of private security, both in the homeland and otherwise. Military hardware and training. Military expertise. Military—"

"Extraterritorial security services?" I feel the urge to help him along. To get to the end. "By private companies?"

"I can't think of a reason why not. And not just extraterritorial. *No no no.* The future of America is in privatization. Private armies of well-paid, middle class men…"

I raise my eyebrows at him.

"…*and* women. The important part: that they be loyalists, focused, with skill sets that are honed to a razor's edge. The skill sets of warriors. But controlled by private concerns." He looks over at me; his eyes are shining yet opaque. "The corporate world is now far more disciplined than the military, my dear. Than the government ever dreamt of being."

"All this seems rather far a field from your background, Howd —I mean, Mandrake." I try to hint, to carefully jog his tortured memory. "Weren't you in financial counseling?"

He ignores me. Howdy lost a passel of money for a whole bunch of folks, and they were so mad at him that one day he just ditched everything he had and came skulking back home. The people were so angry about his oversight in handling their funds that it knocked him completely off center, so much so that ever since he has shuffled around in Grandmother's fuzzy green bathrobe all day and all night, acting like he doesn't remember who he really is anymore. And being glad he didn't end up in jail, or on the wrong end of a firearm, probably. It was a lot of money.

"Far a field. Far, a field. *Far* a field. Far a *field.*" He seems taken with the rhythm of the three syllables, like a poet rolling a line around in his mouth.

He snaps back to the question at hand. "Yes, well, less far from my experience than you might think. I've been doing quite a bit of research."

"So I hear."

Howdy's taken the small inheritance from Grandmother and set up a home theatre in his room, which is where he spends most of his time. With the kind of movies he likes—full of whammies, as he calls the explosions—first I made him reposition the subwoofer, then I gave him money for soundproofing foam, then I finally just moved downstairs into the basement, which is damp but quiet as a tomb. Howdy—the Group Captain—watches movies all night, war movies. I would get Howdy another place to live, with other friends in similar mindsets, but I don't think they'll let him have his movies there. And that would seem cruel and unusual.

The Theatre of Operations. That's what my brother calls his room. It is a lonely space, even when he is in it, like I imagine the sky above must be for God, sitting there by Itself watching the world spin around.

Or maybe It sits there spinning around along with a certain point on the globe, God. Geostationary orbit, somewhere far above Howdy's room. Arthur C. Clarke came up with the idea for use with communication satellites—that, and the space elevator somebody one day ought to build.

All this private mercenary army talk is giving me the willies. Maybe he's been slipping in some CNN with his movie time.

I don't know what my brother does during the day, since I'm out of the house: Somebody has to work around here. If anything, my workday is too short, my summers too long: my students are a vacation compared to Howdy—even when the kids are rowdy. A rhyme in my mind means I have tuned my brother out; it is a nightly event without which I would pout.

I rack my brother back into focus; he is winding it up.

"I think tomorrow is day one," Captain Mandrake concludes with a flourish, dancing the little jig like Hitler in Paris. "I think I have a plan. Wing Attack Plan R, R for Robert. R for Reality. Realities that await to be, to be…"

"Realized?"

He looks dewy-eyed at me. His little sister, now the parent, now the guardian, now the sounding board for his plans to alleviate the onset of doomsday. "*Yes,*" he says with immense gratitude. "Realized, and lived."

And then he floats back up the stairs, his hair all corkscrewed, his slippers too small for his feet, the robe threadbare and ancient. I yawn as I hear the subwoofer thump; what is left of the fire sputters its last bit of cinder-breath before going out once and for all.

AUTHOR NOTE: A winner of the 2008 South Carolina Fiction Project and published in the Charleston Post & Courier, *'Howdy from Upstairs' also features early versions of two key Edgewater County characters, Caughman Howard Shull and his sister Everlynne, who play important roles in the* Dixiana *novel series.*

THE YEAR THEY CANCELED
CHRISTMAS

The frail woman's lukewarm sponge bath, which she welcomed and felt wonderful on her skin, came administered by an attendant. A stranger.

Something on the woman's mind. Her voice quavered, breaking the hollow still of the nursing home. "It's just the awfullest thing you ever heard. Before you know it, they're going to do away with every last bit of it."

The attendant glared flinty-eyed. "Let me guess—Christmas again?"

"I'm-a tell you what."

"Please. Ain't nobody messing with Christmas."

They'll have their way, Flora Mae Harkin warned, after which the holidays would be banished. "Just you wait."

The attendant, large and dark-skinned like all of them on staff at the facility, with names Flora Mae could not remember or even pronounce if her life depended on it, bugged her eyes like one of the comedians on TV. "You think any earthly actor could mess with Christmas? It's the birthday of our Lord and Savior."

"I know what I see on them blaring TVs all day long."

Under her breath, low and mean, and don't think it wasn't

noticed, the attendant warned: "You best not start up with all that mess again today. Enough, now."

Flora Mae, close to ninety, erupted with her own brand of vicious, biting scorn. "I'll start up if I please."

The attendant's hard stare broke, and she chuckled in a sad and pitying manner that rubbed Flora wrong all over again. "Listen, Missus Harkin. When you go to the common area later—and you know the doctor wants you to get up and move around some, if you can—I want you to look all round at that room. And then, I want you to look out yonder on the great lawn, and when I see you later this afternoon I want to hear what you seen in them places."

"What is it I'm looking for?"

"All the decorations—the tree, the wreath on the door. Then try to tell me somebody taking Christmas away. Sometimes I wish they would," she added.

"What on earth do you mean, young woman?"

"I work harder during the holidays than any other time. Trying to put on for my family—the kids, and their little cousins. It supposed to be about relaxing and family, but I tell you what, sometimes I don't know what the holiday season supposed to be about."

Flora Mae grimaced and rolled over with some difficulty. She pulled herself up on one knobby elbow, the brief effort of which seemed to tire her.

"Lay back, now. I'm almost done."

Moaning, she did so.

"So you feel better about all that, now?"

"Christmas." A solitary word, it seemed to scamper over Flora Mae's gums and dry tongue like a spider escaping a hole in a wooden fence, followed by one of its tiny, skittering offspring: "No."

❧

AFTER THE SPONGE BATH, the attendant gave Flora Mae some peace. But once alone, instead of relief she felt only the cold, empty indifference of perpetual ennui, the sun rising and racing across the sky and night again and sun and naps and meals and the bed and the TV. Yes, there were people all around, but it wasn't the same as having family in the house. Folks you could trust.

Maybe Hort would appear this afternoon, as he sometimes did in the waning light, when the red rays of sunset flooded into Flora Mae's room. She dozed all day waiting for that light, which didn't always come. It had to rain sometime, she supposed. And be cloudy. Hort had been gone so long now she was always surprised to see him.

To pass the time she tried to read, but the words in the magazines and that rag of a town newspaper were but a confused jumble. She squinted at the talk shows and the stories on the television for an hour—or longer—but they all were insipid to the point of bland incoherence. She flipped through the channels; the programs she occasionally settled on made precious little sense to her from scene to scene.

She finally let the remote control fall to the floor with a clatter, not caring if she ever used it again. She stared out the window. She breathed in and out, but it was more in service of a sigh than in getting oxygen to her thin blood.

THE NEXT MORNING, Flora Mae decided that as soon as *The Price is Right* went off she'd break up the day by calling her son DeWayne. She figured he would now be sitting at lunch in the diner of the woman named Louella, right there on the town green along with the other few downtown merchants. She wondered, sometimes, if her DeWayne didn't eat at Louella's so often because of its proximity to the town's wretched watering hole, a place of sin and degradation called The Dixiana. Flora Mae Harkin wouldn't have set foot in that awful place even if her hat was on fire and Chief Bolden was standing beside his red fire truck informing her that the last spoonful of water on earth was to be had there inside that sordid honkytonk. She'd burn up, yes she would.

Lord, how that boy of hers drank. There were times all his running around worried her half to death. It was going to catch up with him. Things like carousing always did, one way or another. People either wound up with little babies they didn't want, or sick, or in the ground.

Buzz. Buzz. Buzz.

A tired voice answered. "G'morning, Mee-maw—or afternoon, I reckon."

"Son?" She spoke with a pitiable quaver. "I didn't catch you while you was eating, I hope," she fibbed. She knew if DeWayne was sitting in the corner booth at Louella's in the midst of a broasted chicken basket or an Arkansas Traveler with country gravy, he'd at least be still long enough for her to get a few words out of him. "If I did, I sure am sorry."

"Mama, I love talking to you, but I sure wish we could do it *after* lunch every time instead of during." DeWayne's cadence and tone were dull like an old, tarnished butter knife at the back of the silverware drawer. "This here's the only time I got to myself all day."

"Well, mercy me—I didn't realize the time. What's Louella got good today?"

In response he sounded rote, like a teenage cashier saying *thank you and come again.* "It's Tuesday, so pork chops, flounder, baked ziti."

"Ziti? What's that?"

"Ziti is little pasta tubes, with marinara and cheese."

"*Tubes?*" She sounded disgusted. "I can't halfway understand you, son. I sure hope you ain't been drinking in the middle of the day again."

"Like macaroni. And no, I'm not drinking. Don't know why you'd think I would be."

"Don't you smart off at me," snappish and brusque. "God durn your hide, Horton Harkin."

DeWayne growled at her the way he would when he'd been boozing. "I told you we'd be by tomorrow or the next day for a good long visit, didn't I, Mee-Maw? Now let me eat in peace. Go visit with your friends in that common room. Take lunch in there with all them."

Her heart squeezed and she felt guilt. "I was just wanting to talk to you so much that I didn't *consider* the time."

She held the phone away from her face and cleared her throat of thick mucus—she just couldn't abide it when someone called her and started hacking and bellowing into her ear like a dying bull, so she certainly didn't want to do that to her son. Sometimes Hort would call and start sputtering and going *ack-ack* into the receiver, and when he did, Lord, it made her mad enough to bite a nail in half.

"You feeling okay, today?" he asked.

"I'm just so worried about what all's going on out there."

"What you worried about this time?"

"This whole *Christmas* mess."

Static crackled over the phone. "Mee-Maw," he said, though she heard it each time as *Mama*. "Not that again."

"They just gonna do away with it all this year, finally." Her voice broke. "Like it all ain't bad enough in the world, with them Russians in Cuba and the blacks sitting at the same durn lunch counters as white children and—and—sometimes I think I've just lived too long. Too long for this world."

"The Russians?" He started laughing, the little smart-butt. "They're our friends, now."

"My foot they are!"

"Has a doctor seen you lately?"

"President Eisenhower, no, I mean President *Kennedy*, he was on the TV just the other night and he said, he said—" She smacked her lips, groping for what the President had said. "He said them Russians are piling into Cuba *right now*. Your Daddy is fit to be tied, mister, let me tell you what. Just last night he sat down and wrote a letter to the *Edgewater Advocate* and the *Columbia Record* about it all."

"Cuba. The Russians. Okay. Maybe when I'm there, I can talk to one of the doctors about what's going on with you."

"P'shaw," she sputtered. "Them's the main ones, them rich doctors. You think they give a whit about Christmas, and family? You think they care what it means to celebrate Christmas? They don't give a good god-durn about nothing but them damn golf clubs in the trunks of their Cadillacs."

Golf disgusted Flora Mae; Hort had taken it up after he retired from the power company, spending his golden years playing often with the other reasonably well-to-do old men up at that 'god-durn' country club, as Flora Mae thought of the place. She couldn't stand to set foot in there herself, no ma'am, not with that bunch of snooty old crones worrying about who all sat looking with admiration upon their fine clothes and expensive hairdos.

But then, she'd hated sitting at home all afternoon with nothing but the stories on television for a companion. What was she supposed to do, though? Run up and down the road like a teenager after school? It wasn't dignified.

"Mama," DeWayne said, "I tell you what. I promise I'm gonna come by there tomorrow for lunch. I'll bring us both something good to eat. Something homemade. How's that sound?"

"I'd rather have something from Louella's." She pouted. "That Abby of your'n couldn't find her way around a kitchen stove if her life depended on it."

"Now—that ain't true."

"Is too." If anyone asked her, and they didn't, she thought her son's wife acted like she was too big for her britches. The day DeWayne had walked in with that hussy Abby—wait, wasn't her name Laurie?—and her boobs was a-bouncing around under that T-shirt, Flora Mae knew her baby boy was in trouble.

Then: Flora Mae had no idea why DeWayne even brought Laurie up. Wasn't she dead?

And: Wasn't DeWayne dead, too?

She pish-poshed and p'shawed at her inability to keep it all straight. All these people and names. Must be from watching those lurid TV stories.

Citing his desire to finish lunch and promising a visit like he always did, DeWayne made to ring off.

Flora Mae Harkin reluctantly hung up. She stared at the phone for a while, wondering if it might ring.

It did not.

She wondered if her son drank away his days.

If it all was a lie.

What a lie was.

What 'it' was.

What was.

Next it occurred to call her daughter, but she didn't, because DeWayne's sister Emma Jane wasn't much more sympathetic to Flora Mae's concerns. Emma Jane, like DeWayne, ran around far too much. Peas in a pod.

She hadn't a clue where they'd gotten their wildness from— maybe it was just the times. The world outside Edgewater County seemed to have gone crazy, with men wearing their hair long and women with their bodies on display and those awful wailing guitars in the music, like souls crying out, or demons. Christmas-hating demons.

DeWayne had gone away at Christmas. He'd come back— why, she just talked to him—but when she remembered his voice it made her stomach hurt. She fretted over matters and concerns not under her control.

She worried.

After hours passed—it was only minutes, but to her seemed

much much longer—Flora finally dozed off and before she knew it five o'clock rolled around, and with it time for another bland dinner before *Wheel of Fortune* in the common room.

DeWayne Pullman hung up with his grandmother and felt a grim combination of guilt and annoyance—at certain times he wanted to take his iPhone and chunk it into the Sugeree River.

Instead, he dug back into his cooling blue plate special at Manny's on the Green, which today consisted of pork chops, mustard greens and fried squash. A square of cornbread, a pat of butter half-melted on top; his iced tea sat sweet as pancake syrup. On his third glass, he had been trying of late to break his habit of chewing ice. The food here tasted much better than he remembered when it was Louella's Kitchen.

He chewed ice and mused, waving to people that came and went from the bustling lunch buffet. DeWayne hated being saddled with such responsibility, these daily, confused phone calls. He tried to be a good grandson to his enfeebled forebear, but when they started to slip away like his grandmother obviously had, it was a burden.

If it weren't for him, though, who would pay any attention to the old woman at all? Now that granddaddy was dead, and with DeWayne's no-good mother being the person she was, the responsibility pretty much fell to him. The only other possibilities, an aunt and an uncle who had been quite a few years older than his mom, had also long expired, outlived by their mama in the nursing home. In truth, the man for whom he'd been named had been little more than a shiftless drunk who'd met his end in a car accident that had killed his young wife as well.

All before DeWayne's time; no help.

His no-good mother, another tippling boozehound. It was time for one of his special calls where he attempted, unsuccessfully, to put her in her place. To make her see.

Wouldn't be easy: Shacked up with yet another new lover, this one a well-to-do contractor who lived on a good-sized spread out past the country club, almost all the way over in Chilton closer to the lake country, she said her drinking couldn't be all bad! Look at the big fish this time.

Goody for her, DeWayne thought. Having crested the knoll of fifty, Emma-Jane Harkin's inveterate carousing was the singular aspect of her troubled personality upon which one could count, and maybe this man would at last settle her skinny ass down, at least long enough for her to devote a modicum of time toward dealing with the grandmother issue.

After several rings his mother answered in her froggy, groggy, million-billion cigarette voice; the tone of her scratchy words came as low as that of a burly longshoreman. She hacked and managed to clear her clicking valves.

"Hey there, sugar." *Ack-ack.* "Oh, me. What *time* is it?"

"Mama, you still in bed?" DeWayne, unable to mask his disgust. "It's a shade shy of one o'clock."

"Well, I don't got to keep to no one's schedule, boy." *Ack-ack.* "In particular your'n. You hear me?"

DeWayne said yeah-yeah. Braced against the December wind on the sidewalk in front of Manny's on the Green facing the town monuments, he listened to the clicking of his mother's lighter again and again, her cursing as he supposed she tried getting the first of the day sparked up. "You are your own woman. That much is true."

"Damn straight I am."

DeWayne's gaze settled on the front door of The Dixiana, and at that old codger Rabbit Pettus shuffling in to work the afternoon shift like he'd done for decades, serving the sad old redneck drunks all day, who sat chawing and shooting the poop.

DeWayne ran the back of his hand across his lips and thought about having a quick, cold one, but he didn't drink much any more, not now that he was done with college. His Abby'd kill him if she knew he sometimes sneaked a quick, cold Miller High Life with the oldtimers who hung out during the day at the old honky-tonk. He liked hearing them talk more than the beer itself. Though the beer was good.

The way his namesake uncle had drunk himself to death, though, DeWayne knew he needed to watch himself: They said it ran in families, and the Lord knew his mother presented as yet another familial cautionary tale.

He reflected on his own marriage and the role alcohol had played: while he and Abby both grew up in Edgewater County, they hadn't met until at Southeastern University, but then neither in class nor even on campus: it'd been in a bar, an Irish pub down in the Old Market near campus on what they called Pint Night, all the draught beer half price, a tradition among the students of the huge school.

Abby, petite and sweet and dark-eyed, a hair under five feet, so small that in some styles of shoe she could wear children's sizes. Teenage boys were attracted to her, thinking her to be as young as they; old men thought her younger still. DeWayne had loved her since they were both nineteen, ten years ago now. They'd been soused the first time they made love, but it had still been wonderful and perfect and love it had become for real. That's about all the good alcohol had done him, though. The rest? A DUI, a few failed classes, a sense of shame.

And furthermore, he had to be careful around his big boss at the plant, a pious man named Edward E. Knox, who, too, would shit a brick if he smelled booze, especially since DeWayne was considered a golden boy in the engineering department. He was going places, even if it seemed to him by coming straight back to Tillman Falls after college the way he had, he was taking a step backward. But Abby, his lovely and true high school sweetheart, wanted to stay close to her own family, and once you got married, you had to do things the other person wanted you to even if you didn't, really. Even if it involved coming back home. Already.

He didn't mind. He had gotten a good job, at a great starting salary—they were even going to sport him for his master's—and he and his best girl lived in a nice starter home, one of the new ones in a subdivision near the interstate, an enclave of single family homes that sported its own ten-acre, man-made lake. Tillman Falls was a good place in which to grow up, a nice place to live. The power plant, aging, would one day be supplanted by two new nuclear reactors, a multi-billion dollar project bringing new life to the entire county.

Almost everything felt right to DeWayne.

Almost.

"Well, what is it, son? You don't need no money, I hope." He could hear his mother exhale smoke, could imagine the blue cloud and the shafts of sunlight through a window—the image a familiar one that'd accompanied all his childhood breakfasts, at least the ones his mother arose in time to experience alongside her boy. "'Cause I ain't got none right now. And I can't ask Wade."

"If I needed money, you think I'd ask you? Really."

His daddy Kirby had some money, though DeWayne had tried hard not to ask his dad for help, even though such assistance had been offered to him on numerous occasions. Kirby Pullman had done well with the stationary store, which is what they used to call places that sold office supplies. These days Kirby lived in fear of something like Office Depot opening up near the highway, out where the home improvement store and Hampton's car dealership were located, and DeWayne knew his father spent his days worrying about going out of business and having ten more years until Social Security started. Not enough call for office supplies in a place like Edgewater County, though.

DeWayne and his dad were good friends; they always had been. After the way his mother had behaved, how could he not have sided with his father?

"Mama—you going to see Mee-Maw today?"

"Nuh-uh." She *ack-ack*ed. "Why?"

DeWayne explained in measured tones how the eldest of their family line had called him—again—and that he couldn't abide being the caretaker, not when it was his mother's job to do so. She didn't work, for god's sake, but he didn't need to point that out. Not again.

Emma Jane Harkin, having none of it. "I ain't got time to be traipsing back and forth up Highway 79 every day waiting on her. What we paying all that damn money for?"

"You don't mind riding over and sitting your ass on some bar stool all night. Every night."

She told him to mind his damn business. To get his butt off his shoulders. Like he was better and smarter than her. He wasn't. She said this.

"Mama—I know it ain't easy. That she's not the same. But it's getting to be Christmastime."

Emma Jane fell quiet but for clearing her throat. "I know it is. I know."

"She ain't gonna be around forever."

"Ain't none of us is, son." She laughed, *huh-huh-huh*, as though the acknowledgement of their shared mortality an ironic joke. "We all going to the same place."

Hah, thought DeWayne. Keep believing that.

Enough. "Lookit, don't you worry your little peabrain about her, or anything—you just keep on with whatever you're doing, just like you always done." At moments of high stress his voice broke like that of an adolescent, though it only seemed to happen when he was talking to his no-good mother. He stopped himself from calling her a slut and a drunk—self-evident, this. "I'll go. I'll take her some decent food. It's what she keeps asking for."

He endured his mother's standard speech, coming after her aghast and aggrieved response to the impertinence of being called a peabrain. "Ever since you come back from that damn University, you walk around like your shit don't stink. Well it does, son. You ain't better than me."

DeWayne, ending the call with a trembling touch of his index finger to the screen, its protective layer smudged by pork chop grease: *bloop.*

Going to his car, he realized he'd been holding his ribs tightly, as he had done back when he was nervous while taking exams. He didn't know why it was all getting to him today—nothing ever seemed to change with his mother. If any of this was new or a surprise, he'd like to know how.

EMMA JANE COBBLED TOGETHER a second Bloody Mary, l'il stronger, and smoked her third cig and lolled around on the big bed and looked out the big windows at the big backyard for a while. She flipped through a hundred channels or so on the widescreen television, skimmed through an out of date *In Touch* magazine, chortling with derision at the antics of crazy old Britney Spears and Lindsay Lohan, as well as one of the rich, dumb Durango twins, Maddie or Vangie, the one who was getting so skinny she looked like a living skeleton climbing in and out of her New York City limousines, her head and feet way too big for her sticklike body.

Ice clinked in her glass, and the sanguinity of her bevvie became diluted. She smoked and yawned and took a Zantac, one of Wade's. She washed it down with ice water. It made her stomach hurt worse than the vodka.

Cold, clear water. Making her stomach hurt. Well, if that didn't beat all.

She scoffed, thinking about what her son had said. She had herself another BM, a hair-of-the-dog bracer that was more M than B. Now two-thirty, she knew she had time to go to the nursing home before Wade got home, but couldn't bear the tiresome burden and challenge presented by the drive over there. She'd go tomorrow.

Emma Jane went downstairs into the shimmering beautiful

kitchen which'd been left a bit of a mess—dirty plates stacked on the island and in the sink, skillets, pots, like a pack of college students living there. Wade's ex-wife had been an accomplished decorator and cook, real handy in that way, but since the day Wade had caught her with a mouthful of his business partner's high hard fella in the back seat of her Ford Expedition, it had been Wade's beautiful kitchen, and his alone.

Wade had called his discovery the moment for which he'd been waiting, ten long years since he'd decided he didn't love the hag anymore. Said he didn't care how many guys came in her mouth, worth it to be rid of the nagging ninny. Said for all he cared a hundred rednecks could take turns unloading their wads up her chocolate slide, making the filthy thrusting motion and bugging his eyes and lips out and making a real show of it, espe-cially down at the bar when he really got going. "Have the bitch," he would yell, roaring with laughter. "Go to town, boys." Why he kept bringing all that up, she hadn't a clue.

Emma Jane belched and said hey-hey, lighting another cigarette and thinking that she liked Wade's moxie and big way about everything, even how he put down his ex. Wade Bonner? Oh, yeah—she planned to hold onto Wade like a wide receiver catching the big pass in the last few seconds of a tie game. Despite what her smart-mouth son thought, she was no dummy. Here was a gal who wasn't getting no younger, though on most days she managed to avoid admitting it, keeping on rockin' and rollin' and partying hard as any kid. Hard as she always did. Word to that.

On most days. Sometimes the word was shit.

She suffered some guilt here and there about things that she might or might not have done through the years, yeah she did, but drank it all away. Her mother's precipitous downturn in the last few months hadn't helped much—half the time the old bitch didn't know her, and that only made it worse because now Emma Jane'd never get the chance to have her one and true and final say over slights and insults and other grievances. Not and have it matter. The more her mother had said no, the more Emma Jane had had to prove herself capable of deciding whether yes the better answer. And doing so, again and again. Deciding. Nobody'd ever taken advantage of her, but, boy howdy, what she had wrought through so many little boy-hearts.

In retrospect, it seemed that she'd made her journey of discovery with a hundred different lovers: She dated them from Byrnes High School and the Tillman Military Academy and from as far away as places like Andrew Jackson and Spring Valley, which was near Columbia; yes, she dated them, but Emma Jane did oh-so-much more than just date. She did anything that those boys wanted, and liked doing it. Liked messing around with dicks, liked comparing them—a wide range! astonishing—and reveling in the effect she had on them and their owners.

By her junior year she'd acquired a real reputation; by her senior year, she'd not only gotten an abortion over in Columbia, but had also been in an alcohol-related car accident that had killed the driver, a boy to which she'd been giving a handjob as he raced down old and twisty River Ridge Road, and which ought to have broken her neck as well but hadn't, and for which the Harkins had been oh-so grateful, Emma Jane none the least. *God looks after drunks and little kids*, someone once said; Emma Jane lived her life by that credo, then as now. It hadn't worked out that way for her brother, but that was another story.

As for her sister Nadine, they had been close, but then she got cancer and died at forty-two. And that was that for Emma Jane having any living family members who cared.

She marked the passage of time by the wrinkles on her face, by the dryness of her womanhood even in moments of ostensible arousal, by the shaking of her hands and the ever-worse hang-overs, by the spider veins and circles of callous on her narrow heels, which accumulated with each passing year like rings inside a tree stump and that the grunting Vietnamese (or whatever the hell they were) pedicurist could scrape with an iron file till bloody, it seemed, and would be dry and crusty again in a day, especially in the winter and the last thing she wanted were crusty old woman's heels propped up on big Wade's shoulders.

Time. More and more, stacking up in the corners and recesses of her soul. Time could fuck itself—now, another Christmas was coming up, which meant another year over and done.

New Year's—now, there's a depressing holiday for you, Emma Jane said to no one: the start-all-over holiday. January, definitely the saddest month. Always lists to make and crud to fix. Hard stuff to fix. Impossible. What had time given her but problems and issues and no-good asshole men coming and going, literally, and now another bracer and flipping through to catch the last few minutes of Oprah. On top of all that? An old crone, withering and pestering people on the phone.

A wave of nausea rolled through Emma's stomach. She prayed her mother would pass on peacefully, and soon. She puked up into the back of her throat a little bit. She swished around some of the ice water, swallowed. She belched sharp against the back of her throat, but no acid-puke this time.

She wondered if she shouldn't have stayed married to Kirby, who was a good enough man, if a bit of a dullard. That had been her one shot at settling down, at giving up on her life of 'running around' as her mother had put it with such disdain—but that shot was blown but good, and a long time ago at that. She'd fucked and sucked her way through the marriage as though she were still a single girl, getting it whenever and wherever she could—humiliating, if only he knew the true extent. How many whom her ex still numbered as colleagues or friends. Oh, the shameless and feckless lot of them. The only surprise had been just how long it had taken poor, dumb Kirby to figure out what was going on right under his nose. She felt love and pity for her husband. Missed him sometimes. He would cook for her.

She fixed another bracer, stared out into the sloping backyard toward the pine barren lying beyond. Emma Jane pondered whether she could get away with skipping the visit to the nursing home after all. The old woman probably wouldn't notice anyway.

How much longer, now, Mama? How long? Everybody's got shit to do. We're all still young.

~

THE DAYS—WEEKS?—WENT by, the children still didn't call or visit like they should, and Hort was gone most of the time too, spending every minute, or so it seemed to Flora Mae, out on the damned golf course shaving points off his handicap, whatever that foolishness meant.

Men and their games! And when he wasn't on the links, he sat there in the chair across from her, smacking his lips and sucking his teeth and clearing his throat, every god-durn habit of his that drove her straight up the wall. Hort.

In spite of it all, though, on most days she was glad to see him —he was all she had, after all, besides the colored girls who looked after her, and it wasn't as though she could think of *them* as family, for heaven's sake. But still, she got so fed up in those moments when he became irritated with her over the whole business about Christmas. Hort, pooh-poohing her like everyone else did.

He sucked his teeth and rocked back in the chair. His legs crossed, one pale calf exposed by a pant cuff that had gotten hiked up. Hort had become as thin as a rail, but for most of his life he'd always been strapping and robust, at least prior to his seventieth birthday. All that hoofing around at the country club had made him skinny.

"One of these years, it's just going to be over and done with," she finally said, trying to get his attention before his form faded into the coming dusk.

"What is, sugar?" He rattled his paper and cleared his throat.

"*Christmas.*" She pounded her thigh. "Ain't you been listening to me?"

"Mm-hm," he replied with grave distraction. He peered out the window at the fading light. Rattled his paper.

Gone.

Gone off to his club and his game and his buddies.

She supposed.

Gone somewhere. That much for certain.

She p'shawed to herself, flung a gnarled old hand, the fingers drawn by arthritis inward to the scaly palm. "Just go, then—just go, you old son of a bitch."

DeWayne sat at his desk and rubbed his eyes and closed a few windows and threw a pencil up into the drop ceiling, where it stuck among a few others. On the way into work he'd become compelled to drive by the old place—his grandparents' former home—which was now owned by a thirtysomething couple who, like so many now living in the area, both commuted by day to work in Columbia.

The new owners had made all manner of changes and fix-ups to the property. DeWayne was pleased they hadn't started cutting trees down to keep from raking, or digging up shrubbery to keep from having to trim, or other crazy irresponsible nonsense lazy younger people did when they bought old people's houses. DeWayne had always felt older and more mature than his peers, as though he hailed from his grandfather's generation. Men he could admire. Who'd served. Who'd prospered and lived upstanding lives.

DeWayne had sat in his Jeep for almost a half hour, gazing dreamily at the yard, which lay in autumnal slumber; holiday decorations on all the other houses but this one. When he closed his eyes, he could see the vibrant colors of the coming spring, and felt awash in childhood sense memories: the lavender and blue of the hydrangea, the whites and pinks of the azaleas clustered around the oak trees, the brilliant wine-red of the crepe myrtle blossoms, the pansy redbud bushes blooming royal purple. He remembered what seemed like a thousand-thousand warm and carefree afternoons spent there in the yard. He could smell steaks cooking on the grill, as they had on every Sunday afternoon for most of his childhood. After his parents' divorce, he had spent a great deal of time here on weekdays as well; once his own mother had descended into her slack and profligate ways, it had fallen to her parents—and of course DeWayne's own father, who had his own distractions and issues—to take up the slack.

Clinging to the past. Happier times; innocent times. He knew better. You've got to live in the now, a roommate once told him. Even if it sucks.

"Looks like you got a world-class hangover, son." Loris Mullins loomed in the doorway of the office with a Styrofoam cup of the turbid, crappy swill that passed for Sugeree River Nuclear Station cafeteria coffee. "Got a real head on you last night, I betcha."

"What makes you say that?"

"All you young guys party-hardy, don't you?"

DeWayne, sitting up with a start. "I wish, beau. Just a headache. Garden variety."

Loris Mullins may have been DeWayne's superior, but he wasn't a hard-on or a hard-ass or a hard-anything, not like Edward Knox. Loris was an okay guy, a regular guy. He liked DeWayne. Loris was one of the ones who thought DeWayne had a bright future, and far from being threatened by the young man's intellect, DeWayne could count Loris among those pleased by his youthful coworker's potential and knowledge.

Loris sipped coffee. "How's your grandmama doing?"

DeWayne blew out his lips. "Not so good, Mr. Mullins. Not so good at all."

"Well now, I hate to hear that."

"Nothing to be done, of course. Not much of a prognosis other than the old slow fade."

Mullins slapped his hard, ample gut and belched coffee-breath into DeWayne's small office. "After he got sick, them croakers said Daddy wouldn't last six months, but he fought and suffered and hung on for five years. *Five years.* God-aw-mightee if he didn't. Hating every minute, too."

"Really?"

"Sometimes living ain't all it's cracked up to be."

"Were you relieved? When he passed?"

Mullins shot a hard and raw look at DeWayne Pullman. "Shit if I didn't. You know my back hurt, too? Right in the same durn spot where his cancer was growing? It beat all I ever seen." He sipped coffee, changed the subject to a cold snap building into the state from the north, moved on down the hall.

DeWayne considered the semi-lucid conversations he'd had of late with his grandmother, all concerning the wanton ways of her daughter. The ire the two shared for Emma-Jane Pullman neé Harkin's behavior seemed the equivalent, almost, of Loris's phantom cancer pain—a kind of shared-shame and disdain that indeed nettled and yeah, even physically hurt, somehow.

But eff that, he thought. DeWayne no longer cared what his mother did or who knew it or how it reflected on anything. He only needed some help, and so did his grandmother.

"*Hey,* Mama—how ya doin'?" Emma Jane sounded like a New Jersey goombah—they'd spent the entire day and a night drinking and screwing and watching a *Sopranos* DVD set a client had given Wayne at a holiday party. "Whatcha know good?"

Flora Mae's voice came hoarse, barely above a tortured whisper. "Hey, darling. I sure hope you're coming to see me today."

"Mama, it's already nighttime. I can't come *now.*"

"Oh—I sure hate to hear that."

Her stomach twisted and roiled and lapped a brackish tide at the back of her teeth, but Emma Jane felt no less plowed and happy now that her head spun in that fine as wine way, when all felt at peace and anything was possible, which usually came after she got about halfway through the bottle. It had been a whole week, now, and a number of bottles since DeWayne had castigated his mother regarding her behavior concerning her lonesome, dying mother, but, hey, she'd finally called. "I'll come on by tomorrow, or the next day, for *sure*. That's a superduper promise, girlfriend."

"But the next day's Christmas *Eve*," Flora Mae replied, aghast. "I would sure hope that you'd come and see me then, at least. Your daddy's fit to be tied as it is about you young'uns. You know how he gets."

Emma Jane, bewildered. Not so much by the reference to her deceased father, as she had come to expect such remarks from her mother, but by the fact that Flora Mae had asserted that the holidays had all but arrived—was it already the 23rd of December? The happy, pillowy days all rolled into one.

Last night, a blur: She and Wade had gone to The Dixiana for happy hour and shots and beers, and then to eat at the Seafood Shack, where Emma Jane had drunk one-dollar Coors Lights one after another while her boyfriend had gorged himself on buffet popcorn shrimp and crab legs and Coronas; and then home, where they got into a few tall, cold vodka-tonics to help rinse out the grease from the buffet. For some reason, the heat and plenty of the food at the restaurant had made her feel queasy and guilty: Her father had loved eating at that buffet.

"What do you want from me for—for—?" Emma Jane cursed as she dropped her cigarette. She bent over to pick it up, but the cherry had been knocked off, which along with an empty glass and the need to get off the phone presented another shitty development in her lousy, happy, pillowy life. "I mean: what you want from us—Wade and me—for Christmas, sugar?"

Flora Mae's words, now, could be heard more forcefully. "I just want for there to still *be* a Christmas."

"Well it ain't like they gonna cancel it, Mama." Emma chortled at the thought. "You been watching too much Bill O'Reilly, and that other'n. You and Wade both."

"Just you wait," her mother said. "One year, it simply won't come."

"Them assholes on the TV ain't nothing but actors. I don't care if they do call it news."

"That's the silliest thing I ever heard."

"Well—you ought to know, Mama. With all your talk about canceling Christmas."

DEWAYNE AND ABBY had already been in the car on the way to visit his grandmother when the person from the assisted living facility called. The couple had packed along baked goods and gifts and new magazines for the common area, the ones Abby brought home from Dr. Williamson's office where she worked as a dental hygienist, magazines she held in her lap, flipping through while DeWayne drove.

And then the phone rang.

The couple, already terrified and elated at the news they carried—that very morning Abby had peed on the strip, and the two bars had appeared—both reacted with grief at the report that Flora Mae, her vital signs low, appeared to be dying. They wanted to tell her, DeWayne's Mee-Maw, the news as a sort-of Christmas gift, one sure to buck up his grandmother's spirits—not only were her unseen malefactors demonstrably *not*, in fact, getting rid of Christmas, but now he had the most magical message of all: The gift of life. Knowledge that the wheel would continue to turn. No more comforting notion, he assumed, for a woman of her age and condition.

Not simply a woman—a mother. A grandmother. Without her, no DeWayne. The reason for the season.

He'd been grinning from ear-to-ear when the phone had blipped at him, a siren-like ringtone he'd assigned to the nursing home number. He steered with one knee and cursed and rang off with them. Speeding them down the graying asphalt of Highway 79, Abby said what's wrong what's wrong slow down, and he explained.

He called his mother. Didn't get her. Left a message, bitter and panicked and shrill. His words had rung in his ears. "Mama, damn your ass. Pick up the motherfucking phone."

By the time they got there, his grandmother had gone, gone away: a frail husk left lying under the sheet, a cottony shrouded chrysalis bearing away the remains of his forebear. DeWayne wept, not with relief at being free of her, but in grief for that childhood spent with this woman. His true mother, as he'd considered Flora Mae Harkin.

"Everything good about me came from you and Pa-Paw," he said, weak with grief. Abby put her hand on his shoulder, comforted him best she could.

Following her much-delayed and elaborate, loud arrival in the nursing home lobby, at the sight of her mother's body Emma Jane wailed and pretended to faint down on the floor, and if it wasn't an act DeWayne would be damned.

In the hallway outside his grandmother's room, DeWayne foreswore Abby not to tell his mother about the baby—never to tell her. Wouldn't allow it, he said in a hushed, rage-filled threat.

Abby had looked frightened of DeWayne, maybe for the first time. He would have to explain later. He would take back that look he'd had, that feeling of anger and violence. He'd put it away, like they were going to bury his grandmother, in the cemetery there next to her husband. After which DeWayne would deal with his mother. Would put her someplace, too—in her place, if nothing else.

Wait—the baby. Not telling her, that was it. Wrapped in a nutshell. The ultimate. DeWayne laughed, dark and wicked and mean. Last laugh, he thought.

⌓

THE CELL PHONE went off with its distorted ringtone, a low-fidelity version of the chorus from 'Margaritaville' that startled Emma Jane into a half-heart attack—as she stumbled out of bed and over to the dresser where her phone lay buzzing, her squeezing little ticker pounded and went flippy-floppy in her chest, the skin wrinkled and peeling from where she'd lain out during that warm spell last week and gotten a sunburn.

SON, the readout informed.

Her head swimming, the little glowing screen doubled and tripled. She didn't answer.

He left a VM. DeWayne sounded mean as a snake, telling her to get her ass over to the nursing home and that Mee-Maw was slipping away.

"That old hussy. Just like her to pull some shit like this at Christmas."

Emma Jane staggered down the hallway, naked, toward the kitchen. Bashed her little toe on the leg of an occasional table one of Wade's grandbabies had pulled out from the wall last time that crazed brood was running roughshod over the house. Mercy, but his daughter had cut her eyes at Emma Jane the whole time, snapped at her the way DeWayne always did, and maybe it was something about their whole smart-ass little generation.

"Damn you," she barked at the silent phone. "I told you the other day I was going over there later with fruitcake and Mama's present, didn't I?"

She shook her head at the time, at her condition, and at the supposed news from her worry-wort son. Wade had his grandbabies coming over later, and both were sure to be on a holiday rampage.

A nightmare, in other words. Emma Jane had such a head on her today. And now this.

As she surveyed the wrecked kitchen, she was stunned to see that the half gallon of Grey Goose vodka they'd bought only two days prior sat on the granite countertop quite devoid of ethanol but for a trace. She had no memory of even coming back to the house the previous night. She felt a vague soreness 'down there,' which meant she and Wade had gone at it, but she had no clear recollection of such activity. Not only was he as big as a horse, but when he was drunk it sometimes took him up to an hour to finish. They'd go at it every which way he could think of, spinning her around and handling her and pushing and moaning and thrusting, pausing to turn on porno, giving him head for a while, fighting him off about getting himself backdoor action, which with a doorknob like his was like, no way, José.

Then, the headache thrummed into life, the bile lapped into the back of her throat, and she no longer required specific memories to fill in the facts of her behavior—she gagged and puked into the stainless steel sink she always forgot to Comet out at the end of the cleanup, and over which Wade would yell at her and call her a dumbshit cow who couldn't keep a kitchen if she tried, and that if she weren't a good lay she would have been on the street a long time ago, but that wasn't him that was the booze and afterwards he would cry sometimes and fuck her silly and none of it mattered, not even when he pushed her down and slapped her that one time. A big man with a big dick and a bigger, harder slap across her face, and she'd gone end over end and bonked her head on the step and had had double vision ever since, but hadn't told anybody.

She gagged and heaved again, into a film of greasy bits of salmon and avocado and beans from the Southwestern meal Wade had put on for her while she made drinks and laughed and shot pool on table, and looked out at the lake best she could through her vibrating double vision.

Recovering, she lit a cig and plopped down on a stool by the kitchen's breakfast bar, her heart flipping and flopping again. She got herself together as best she could—she smoked the cigarette, sat with her head in her hands, trembled, felt ill, tried to drink water, but started coughing and ended up spitting it up all over Wade's wife's sink again. A good start on cleaning it, which she would need to do after getting herself together and before she rode over to the nursing home.

She thought about a bracer, and went to get some orange juice, just a swallow or to to complement the swallow or two in the bottom of the vodka bottle—a bit more, really, almost a finger, which in that half-gallon would make one or two little bracers, and maybe eat herself a pack of Nekot cookies or Nip-Chee crackers. That would put a decent enough stomach on her to make a drive.

Later, she would come back and help Wade feed everyone. And clean out the sink. She would not forget, even if they got to the bottom of another big handle of vodka tonight, which if people came over they might and would and could. She'd scrub it till it shined. She had to—Emma Jane couldn't lose Wade.

She went into the master bathroom. Wade was still passed out flat on his back like he'd been for hours, snoring like a rusty lawnmower. His thing stuck up like a flagpole under the sheet. A man-machine. She felt raw at the thought.

Her complexion, sallow—without her make-up, she looked sixty going on dead, shriveled from all those days spent laying out, the years writ large across her face. Years and lines and nights gone by, oh my.

She thought about it being Christmas, and about her brother DeWayne up in heaven, her sweet baby brother for whom she'd named her own sweet sweet baby boy. God, how she had looked up to DeWayne when she was little. The year he got killed, Christmas had been the worst one she could ever remember, except maybe the first one after the divorce, when she had had to drop her baby off at Kirby's house and just leave him there to have his Christmas morning apart from his mommy.

Dizzy again, she sat down on the toilet, holding her temples with the thumb and forefinger of her right hand. She would take a couple of Tylenol, lie down for a while. Maybe shower. Try to eat those crackers, and have those bracers and get on her way. She had time; her mother had been dying for ages. Surely the old coot would wait until after Christmas to go, especially since the holiday was such a big fricking deal to her.

AUTHOR NOTE: This *multi-generational, multiple POV Southern family drama never found a publication berth other than on* Edgewater County Confidential, *but remains one of my favorite short stories.*

FAITHLESS ELECTORS

By the time the primaries, contentious as they might have been, finally offered a conclusive, ironclad result, the campaign year found itself in full, unified swing:

Turtlechurch, the product to be rolled out.

Turtlechurch, the great unifier.

Turtlechurch, the name to be whispered upon the wind between now and November, over and over and over until *Turtlechurch* became synonymous with the concept of *foregone conclusion*.

A blessed event. The coming of the savior.

"We're all relieved to see a frontrunner of such stature and certitude," as network newsreader Cynthia-Anne Goforth put it. "The choice—which of course is still yours to make—nonetheless seems clear."

There it was: Eugene Turtlechurch, with his wife Beatrice—as powerful an American couple as could be imagined, known and respected far and wide for their stupendous accomplishments—held the best shot at unseating the incumbent.

In fact, Beatrice made the ticket as formidable as any running mate Eugene would later choose: an Ivy League scholar and full partner in a rock-star law firm that had defended—and gotten off scot free—no fewer than three spouse-murdering celebrities, a politician caught with his pants down and money sticking in his hole, and a kid who shot up the grammar school cafeteria over a girl that had broken up with him (a tough sell), Beatrice cut quite a media figure.

In a further, incestuous little wrinkle, Beatrice had even defended the current Leader of the Free World her husband sought to unseat, Bertolt Bednap, an avuncular African-American who, after being accused of selling military secrets to the Chinese, had suffered impeachment for high crimes and generally treasonous behavior. With Beatrice Turtlechurch as lead counsel, the House failed to convict, of course. At the press briefing following the vote, Bednap called Beatrice "a true American patriot," and later, before an exultant joint session of congress, bestowed upon her the Universal Medal of Truth and Freedom.

Beatrice Turtlechurch—they called her The Eater of Worlds —possessed a shock of flaming red hair, steely-cold, impenetrable eyes, and, at forty-five, a body for which most women of any age would give their eye teeth. She ranked way, way up there in the annual most-admired-women polls that all the newsmagazine websites conducted. Her oatmeal cookies were renowned, her meat loaf recipe even more so. She regularly appeared on talk shows and podcasts and youtube channels; she did a wide-open beaver shot session for *Hustler*, and the times being what they were, received praise for having done so—the rumor went around that they hadn't even needed to Photoshop any physical flaws on her body. She symbolized the modern American woman in a manner about which her colleagues and rivals could only dream. Her husband seemed to worship the ground over which her power-heels floated. Ostensibly, at least, she eschewed obfuscation.

Beatrice represented the best of what her generation had to offer. Perhaps even more so than the candidate himself, as more than one member of the commentariat had opined. But hey, as the charming Eugene was wont to say: you've got me, and now you're stuck with me.

More than any of them realized.

In any case, Goforth had been right: the time of Turtlechurch seemed upon the world. Or so Eugene himself had been informed.

∾

BUT FOR ALL HER ACHIEVEMENTS, Beatrice, as her husband knew so well, represented only one-third to one-half of the equation: Eugene Turtlechurch, now, here was a star in the grandest and most obvious sense, and had been since before Beatrice had even gone to Harvard Law School way back in the Naughty-Naughts.

Had been groomed for it. Perhaps even bred:

Eugene had cut his EPP (Extreme Public Persona) teeth as a child YouTube star turned game show host turned novelist turned movie star turned distinguished talk radio über-wag turned activist for the relief of third world debt turned all-around media supersensation. His game show *Piss Up A Rope* featured ordinary, untrained laypeople competing for prizes by performing delicate urological procedures on unsuspecting patients. His best-selling novel *The Pigfucker Chronicles* (*New York Times Review of Books* blurb: "Finding intrigue and unlikely romance among the entrails, amateur sleuth Atwater St. Rove investigates a series of slaughter-house murders"; the novel's ghostwritten sequel—*The Other White Meat*—had been coolly received, and this despite being mostly pictures rather than text) was optioned and made into a multi-season streaming series that included an important cameo by Turtlechurch himself. Thusly re-launched on a career as a reborn Hollywood celebrity, a status of high public interest that persisted for well over a year, the foundation of Turtlechurch's political ambitions were set in 200-ton blocks of limestone as solid as the base of an ancient Egyptian pyramid.

By the time the game show was canceled and the movie deal fell through and the last book remaindered, however, Turtlechurch dropped off people's radar screens for a news cycle or three. Later, he recovered with the talk show gig and his phony PR campaign to help starving brown people, a notion that had had real play during the ephemeral Compassion Craze that gripped the nation for a few hours in the midst of the cold winter of '25.

Turtlechurch finally made the leap into politics by entering a nationally-watched Senate race in a state from which he had not hailed, but still garnered wide public support after the sole televised debate, during which he'd physically assaulted his rival, an American-born ethnic female named Napthalia Sanganeer. The determined and unrepentant act of violence—"Who's your daddy *now*?" he'd screamed as he wailed on the diminutive female opposition candidate with a concealed cudgel, beating her bloody and senseless—transformed him into a more formidable megastar than he'd ever been.

Fame—world fame.

From that high water mark he had been propelled upon the shoulders of adoring constituents to the august Senatorial body from his adopted home of New New York, besting the incapacitated and hospitalized incumbent by nearly fifty percentage points. Even though Eugene would go on to serve only a fraction of his first term, people all over the continent declaimed that he was the kind of leader they'd not simply been waiting for, but for which they had hungered as ravenously as snowbound, abandoned livestock trapped in a Nebraskan blizzard.

After serving in DC for approximately three and half weeks, he'd announced his intention to form a committee to explore the likelihood of victory in seeking the round office, and ever since had run an endless and totes legit campaign for the big chair. Every press conference during the Bednap impeachment had featured him standing in the background behind Beatrice Turtlechurch and at the side of Bednap, a dovetailing of imagery that had served them both handsome dividends. All of it—the politics stuff—had given Eugene a taste for the big-time like that boy had never known. Which was sayin' something.

OUT ON THE STUMP, Eugene Turtlechurch presented as a rhetorical dreadnought: unstoppable, unflappable, sharp as a tack and twice as quick and witty as any partisan heckler; fine sprays of spittle flecked from his flapping lips. A beautiful, fit man who stood stock-straight and whose teeth flared white, skin crisped to a healthily amber tan meant to evoke Bednap's skin tone, and whose wardrobe hung with a cut and drape that was fashionable without seeming ostentatious. He had more money that any one man could possibly need. A robust fifty-three, he claimed he was forty-nine, but could have passed for thirty-eight. It was whispered—hell, shouted—that he possessed an absolute monster of a schlong.

During his barn-burning campaign stops, Turtlechurch had a way of making the crowd believe not only that great things were possible, but outright miracles could be had in exchange for the right brand and quality of loyalty. His cogent discourse flowed as the perfect marriage of grandiloquence and simplicity; he acknowledged and drew out people's deeply held beliefs in ways that made them seem concrete, but also evoked palpable terror of the unknown in a manner gut wrenching, yet manageable:

"They won't attack us *again* with nuclear weapons, not on *MY* watch," he thundered at a certain, carefully considered point. "By the time I'm through speaking at the UN? They'll *all* be too busy shitting themselves bloody with fear to do our way of life any real harm, and I'm talking our friends, too, not only our enemies. We'll surround those shiftless, beady-eyed fucks—all of them—with everything we got. We'll cut off their dicks and grill them with onions and peppers and garlic and serve them on hoagie rolls at the State Fair with horseradish and slaw. SLAW," he would yell before whispering: *"We'll make them sorry they chose to wander out of their dusty, stinking spider-holes."*

But this, the big finish. He opened his campaign appearances by bursting onto the stage and dance-vamping with his straw boater (everything old is new again—most of the men in his audiences, from all walks of life, sported the hats as well) and wielding a prop-cane he spun around like Gene Kelly in an old movie musical nobody remembered. He sang an inspirational song of his own composition, juggled three objects given to him at random from audience members (who were actually Secret Service plants, of course), and led the audience in an obeisant prayer to Jesus Christ. Next, he told a lengthy, ribald joke that, following the uproarious punch line, allowed him to use the premise of the witty tale to illustrate a point of contention regarding, say, the Social Security insolvency crisis or the War Against Reasoned Thought or the Fukushima Radiation Controversy, topics about which much ink and blood had been spilled.

His ultimate promise? "You put me in charge of this little concentration camp of ours, and I'll fix everything."

"Really?" one of the plants would call out. "But—*how?*"

"Details are for the interns. Besides, would this face lie to you people?"

"No," one of the other plants would call out.

Leaning forward and cupping an ear: "*Would it?*"

"NO," came the refrain from the vibration of ten-thousand throats.

"Bless your hearts, every one," his voice breaking on cue. "I won't let you down."

His followers responded in kind to his enthusiasm and optimism: They cheered and stomped their feet and threw boaters in the air until the candidate would shush them. Right then he'd lean in, whispering with conspiratorial glee, "Now, let's not start shucking each other's corn just yet." After that line the crowd would cheer and stomp and throw the hats some more as he screamed out, "'Cause I'm a-tellin' ya we got us a *mess* of work to do, people! A mess of work to make this here place uh-great a-gain!"

Grown men wept and women fainted. Children, coached

beforehand, clasped their hands and knelt at the foot of the stage. Eugene had them, every one. Not that their votes mattered.

BEHIND THE SCENES, though, Eugene Turtlechurch was already running out of gas. With the national campaign only halfway over, this was like, a freaking problem. He'd need new gimmicks, new gags, new material, new medication if he were to make this long season work in his favor.

No one but him knew how burned out he truly was—no one but Beatrice, that is, but she didn't appear to be concerned.

After a rally in which Eugene had tried out a new joke that had fallen flatter than the GNP had been for the last three or four decades—the crickets he heard in response caused him to go backstage and strangle the head writer with one of Eugene's own bow ties—he stormed into his hotel suite and cracked a popper under his nose to be able to feel again.

Feel. Anything. At all.

His aide-de-camp Richard Pullen, narrow fingertips flicking at bits of lint, took Eugene's tweed suit-coat and hung it in the closet, afterwards standing at a tortuous semi-parade rest to await instructions. Pullen's hunched demeanor and wrinkled topcoat made him appear like a six-foot, crumpled brown lunch sack. It had been a long campaign. Pullen, in his 60s, had been one of Turtlechurch's handlers going all the way back to the YouTube days.

"Dick, you look like someone just sold you a bag of shit they'd advertised as chicken wings. Out with it, bud."

"Well—Mrs. Turtlechurch awaits. Downstairs."

Eugene made a face as though he'd bitten into one of those metaphorical fried turds. "Why in god's name is she in Boise—I mean, Des Moines? What about the Women's Right to Vote Against Their Own Interests rally tomorrow in Fargo?"

"Canceled."

"And the meet & greet with the deformed adult children of Iraqis we hired back in the Naughty Naughts to collect depleted-uranium bomb casings from around the Green Zone?"

"Negatory, chief—she cleared the schedule. Said we'd better 'get our heads out of our asses, and not yesterday, either'."

"Christ in a sidecar. She said it like that?"

"You did hear the quote marks in my tone. I hope."

Undeniable.

Eugene sputtered about the necessity of keeping the tight, carefully considered agenda, of hitting the right markets, of watching the polls as the race tightened—or not, as the case might be—and finally about how, if everyone didn't settle down, it could be time for a shakeup on the campaign staff.

"A shake-up? To what end?"

"That Bednap's a mako shark." Eugene, fretting. "We can't let our guard down."

"Well, I wouldn't be completely against some new blood." Pullen, catty, a sly look on his pinched, untrustworthy features. "But those ravenous dogs in the press, why, they'll claim you're unstable. That you can't keep a team together. That you couldn't steer a garbage scow around New New York harbor. That you're a craven, pusillanimous, flatfooted figure-finagling fussbudget—"

Eugene charged across the room as though onstage at one of his rallies and grabbed his aide by the throat. "What are you talking about? We own the press."

Pullen gurgled, "True-dat."

"More to the point: why the hell is Beatrice downstairs?"

"Let me go."

Turtlechurch did so. "Sorry."

Coughing and clearing his throat, Dick Pullen explained that Mrs. Turtlechurch had been informed of her husband's fatigue and creeping ennui. Decided to come see for herself. "She has as much riding on this as you."

"Very well. Bring in the future first lady."

AFTER A DISCUSSION REGARDING Eugene's issues, Beatrice shook her head and got down to brass tacks: "Our problems are more immediate."

Eugene, skeptical. "In what way?"

Beatrice nodded to Pullen, who explained that with enough of a true-democracy movement left—not much, but some—nettlesome buttmunches could find out how the elites had already presented the candidates with the forthcoming election results: Turtlechurch was to receive a staggering 81% of the popular vote, and corrupt but charming Bednap would have to make do with a consolation prize of 22%. "Rumors are circulating. That's all I can say."

"Whoa—the foreknowledge thing might cause a bit of a stink."

Beatrice chortled. "Hell, everybody already knows. Anyone who's halfway awake, anyway. In the last national election, the totals actually exceeded the number of eligible voters by a significant margin—and nobody even noticed."

"Anybody who makes too much hay'll find themselves in a reorientation camp, where they belong." Pullen, sparking up a Marlboro Maryjane and holding in the smoke. "Fucking traitors."

But in the end, Beatrice expounded that such allegations could be used to shore up Eugene's support instead of eroding it: should the old saw about fixed elections rear its ugly head yet again, *Crackpot Conspiracy Theory* would be the talking point repeated like a soothing mantra, until everybody forgot about it and moved on to the next distraction.

Beatrice checked her device. "Here's what concerns me: Bednap has more than two-dozen staged mass shootings and terrorist attacks in the offing between now and the election. It could be that we're the dupes in all this. Ever think of that?"

Eugene snapped his fingers. "Soft on terror. That's the ticket."

Pullen, crossing his legs to hide a sudden erection. "Oh, that's good."

Next they went over other concerns, like the activist-dissidents who'd been causing problems. Rare and wraithlike creatures sometimes seen near campaign rallies, these odd, cloaked trouble-makers somehow slipped past the checkpoints and sought to disrupt the carefully constructed theatre that was politics. Eugene couldn't wait to round them all up and put all their troublemaking butts into one of the KBR-managed camps out in the desert. When dissenters came out of one of those places—if they came out at all—t'was with a whole new 'tude 'bout keeping their filthy pie-holes shut regarding human rights and shit.

"Hey." Eugene, brightening. "You know what? Now that we're off the grid for a cycle or two, let's relax. Let's celebrate." He thumbed his needlephone and barked, "Fuel the jet. Cancel every-thing for Wednesday and Thursday. Issue a press release saying I'm going into rehab for forty-eight hours to get my meds regulated."

"Better living through chemistry. They'll eat it up." Pullen, pie-eyed and chill from his weed break. "Not that it matters."

THE TURTLECHURCH CAMPAIGN JET—PAID for by Abercrombie F. Eaglesworth, the richest man in the United Emirates of North America—was a sumptuous G-17 with a lovingly decorated boudoir, a karaoke bar, a jammin' gourmet kitchen and a kickin' VR theatre; essentially, a tragically hip apartment in the sky. The plane's cruising altitude, a not-so-low sub-orbit; if the AI really pushed the old girl into a maximal parabolic flight path, passen-gers could find themselves transiting from, say, Melbourne to Vegas in forty-five, door-to-door.

Today, though, only cruising. The sky glowed a deep, bruised violet color as they arced westward toward a secluded artificial island in the South Pacific, a hideaway constructed atop a rotating mass of plastic grocery sacks and soda pop bottles situated well out of the main radiation lanes from the Japanese reactors that had been leaking for fifteen years. Everybody's tuna was lab-grown now, boy.

Eugene chilled in the bedroom, rapping on the vidilink with Pullen up in the cockpit about the next week's worth of appearances: how the new jokes stunk to high heaven. How the quality of the dance moves Dick's choreographer provided also lacked a certain *je ne se quai*. And how, "If the craft table doesn't hit a more sophisticated note at the next corn-pone town hall meeting, those flyover folk will be gawking at me schlepping into town with my own damn bucket of fried fritters instead of the local fare. And that won't look good, now will it?"

"Don't forget the persona: A regular schmoe, going through the same automats as everyone else. Eating the *people's* food."

Eugene grimaced at the thought of all the times he'd eaten the same food most citizens were coerced into consuming by relentless advertising—and a lack of choice. "Don't remind me."

"Man of the people, mulling the same two choices as everyone else: frankenfish and chicken-lips."

Eugene threw up in his mouth, swallowed it.

Besides, The War on Choice was the campaign slogan of Chancellor-President Bednap, the incumbent Demapublican who, despite Beatrice's masterful courtroom exoneration, Eugene would soon trounce in the grand general election on the first Tuesday after the first Monday, or so it had all been laid out by the central bankers.

The Prez had some snap and style of his own, though. Eugene had to give him that.

For instance: Choice, Bednap declaimed in his top hat, tails, and blinding white spats, presented in many ways as the enemy of the people: "Who hath the time to wade through the endless alternatives so plaguing many of us and our parents, going back into the last century? No, no, no." Bellowing and squinting through his gleaming monocle: "More choices are not the answer—*fewer is more.*"

Eugene, admitting that Bednap had himself a campaign slogan with pizzazz, took a long look in the mirror and checked his privilege. "How are the pizzazz numbers looking?"

"Pizzazz you ain't gots to worry about. They're higher than this Eagleberry Corporate jet in which we're cruising, oh great one."

Eugene rang off and stretched. But it wasn't all flash and pizzazz, not exactly. Folks existed who were still interested in the issues facing humanity like longtime survivability of the species, that type of nonsensical, far-off, gloomy, hysterical razzmatazz. Eugene's platform, a single page, offered the suggestion he possessed a go-zillion point plan for this and that problem; they just had to drive a basic idea into the collective head of the elec-torate—hope. Hope that a savior with a decent tailor and a cheerful outlook had come along to clean up the mess.

The American dream—somebody else cleans it all up.

"Bea?" Eugene, in sock feet, easing into the main cabin. "A drink?"

"Is there time?"

"We still have a few minutes before landing."

"Why not."

Beatrice grimaced and gripped the sides of a plush captain's chair while her coolie, a young Syrian girl with chubby cheeks who looked terrified as all get-out, completed a rigorous pedicure. Beatrice's shocking red wig lay in the other chair across from the girl; its violent coloring complimented the bands of sunset outside the portal. Without the wig and makeup, Beatrice appeared on the leeward side of seventy.

To the servant she barked, "What are doing down there, major surgery?"

"Your feet very rough," the girl replied in a cowed, accented whisper. "You do not have mani-pedi often enough."

"I'm in the middle of a god-damn presidential campaign. I have to wear come-fuck-me's in a cornfield. Do your worst."

"Honey, can you do anything about the odor?" Eugene, howling as he mixed a pair of tall, frosty Betty Fords. "The paint in her shoe closet is peeling."

Beatrice flipped him off. "Just serve up the brine, Ho-Jon."

"Coming right up, *Mis-sus Prez-i-dent*," Eugene sang in a bright melody signaling his pleasure at all things Beatrice.

Eugene had his own personservant for such mundane matters as drink making, but these days one couldn't be too careful, and of late he preferred handling his own liquor. He'd been informed that one of the hooded protesters had infiltrated the White House as a coal shoveler, and adulterated Bednap's fresh-squeezed GMO grapefruit juice (brand name: *Joosh*). Thankfully, the tasters had discovered the mickey in time.

Also, a sure-bet candidate several election cycles ago had ended up replaced after someone—yes; an investigation revealed it was another of those pesky cloaked dissidents—spiked a cigar she'd been given at a South Carolina stump meeting with *rabbit tobacco*, as the additive was known on the street. A powerful organic hallucinogenic herb, after ingestion the victim lost control of her mind for about a day and blurted nothing but the truth. This made the substance a dangerous, dangerous scourge requiring governmental action, even though the plant from which it was refined occurred naturally, and thus had to have been a part of God's plan. The authorities argued, however, that God, typically infallible, had screwed the pooch with this one plant. The assertion sounded reasonable enough to most folks.

This latest drug crisis had engendered an effect on the general population as well, fomenting a plague of introspection and rampant self-actualization, concepts that poll after poll had shown to be troublesome, if not downright appalling, to the elites controlling the course of human history. The subsequent crackdown on users had been brutal and sustained; rabbit tobacco enthusiasts were now classified as a new breed of seditious terrorist, and to be put away for life, if not executed.

The unfortunate, failed candidate in question, Busbee Muckenfuss, had been observed the morning after being dosed with rabbit tobacco taking a massive, liberating dump smack in the middle of the tarmac beside her campaign plane, after which she lurched around the runway with her pantyhose still bundled around her ankles, flinging her own feces at her security detail in a most playful and amused manner while declaring through a bullhorn that the entire electoral process, especially electronic voting machines, represented nothing but a sham and a farce.

The truthtelling part had been bad enough, but amazingly the Muckenfuss handlers found no good way to spin public defecation. Not yet at least, but a new game show called *Shit On A Shingle*, a pointed scatological reference designed to remind voters of Eugene's own classic quiz show, was scheduled to debut in the fall on the most popular streaming service later, after which talk show hosts had been speculating that shit-slinging just might possibly become quite the craze among the iGen hipster set.

He served the drinks. "This will set you right, Mother—oops, I mean wifey dear." Eugene chugged his cocktail and smashed the glass against the emergency exit doorway, howling like a coyote in heat. "I dumped half a fifth in there."

"All right all right *enough*." Beatrice jerked her foot away from the girl, who'd been sawing at a callous with a gray file. "Finish later."

"Don't pick at it," the girl advised, her head down. "I finish later."

"Is there an echo in here? Get out."

The girl exited toward the front of the aircraft. Beatrice glowered after her. "Ragheads. They're about as good for doing nails as I am for cooking."

"Now, now. Look at what she's up against."

Beatrice fingered her comlink. "Have somebody ice that little twerp for insubordination, would you, Pullen? She offended my religious sensibilities. Issue a press release that indicates she was a deep cover agent from Bednap's campaign who tried to give Eugene chlamydia. It'll engender a sense of melodrama and suspense while we're off the road."

"*Done and done-er,*" Pullen chirped with good humor.

Beatrice, with a scowl. "Gene, what are you doing in here anyway? I thought you were exhausted."

Turtlechurch shrugged. "Just wanted to hang, I guess."

She regarded him with suspicious disgust. "To what end?"

"Talk, maybe?"

"We don't have a meeting scheduled."

"Like real people."

She snorted. "How much liquor have you had?"

Eugene's genial demeanor crumbled. "I'm suffering ennui."

"It's nothing that can't be adjusted."

"No, I'm serious. Here's the thing: I understand how the world works. I do. Otherwise," an aside to himself, "I wouldn't be the chosen one. But it all just lacks—truthiness."

Bored with this already, Beatrice picked at her feet. "One can only hope."

The candidate squinted at the sky, with its exact same hues as before: the aircraft, chasing the sunset. "This game, this part we're playing—you wonder if there's not another way to run the world than this."

"Do tell."

"Like how people used to think it was run. The whole democracy thing."

"That sham? Besides, used-to-be's don't count any more. Those faithless fools barely vote in the first place."

"Word. But still—"

Beatrice, toweling off her rubicund, wrinkled feet. "Turtlechurch, when you get like this I swear you're positively infantile. Existentialist philosophy is for men with diminutive appendages and overlarge frontal lobes—the eternal balance. We both know you're part of the other group, the real men—"

"—and fiercely proud of it—"

"—so it's difficult for me to grasp the value of having these ridiculous discussions. Isn't there a script you should memorize? Stagecraft to be refined? Rhetoric to be polished?"

He couldn't disagree. "But Bea—maybe I want to be a real leader."

"We all signed onto this; you've seen the play-out, as well as the pay-out; and you can no more 'lead' than you can get out of it now without—without—"

"*What?*"

"Without eating the big one. That what you had in mind?"

"I, ma'am, am no John F. Kennedy."

Beatrice, yawning. "Tell me something I don't know."

Eugene paced in a small circle. He tried several times to speak, but no words came.

Finally: "Never cared for that aspect of the contract."

"Now, look here." She slipped the wig over a mottled, bumpy skull covered with wispy tendrils of gray hair, like dust bunnies clustered underneath an antique piece of furniture in an abandoned farm house. "If I didn't think you were the right person to play this part, I'd never have agreed to it. Hell—if I'd held out, it would be me about to close this deal instead of you. But I didn't. Public not ready for a female trial lawyer as leader? *Hah.*"

"Your unlikeables are too high, that's what they said. Trial lawyers—the lowest, right? It's enough of a risk to have put you in this position as it is."

"Granted. Touché." The comlink chirped. "Speak."

"Landing in one minute, ma'am."

Beatrice shot to a standing position. "For pity's sake, you sodding idiots—*get my face people back here.*"

"Right away," Pullen squawked.

THE BRIEF VACATION WENT WELL, although as the hours passed

Beatrice withdrew into a distant shell. Engaging in furtive comlink conversations, she seemed distracted as they plotted out the next few weeks of the campaign. To Eugene, all of it felt like an exercise, one holding a perfunctory air.

By himself for once, he reclined on the plastic beach and watched the greasy cobalt blue of the waves lapping against the artificial shoreline. Bored, he rang up his old buddy Bednap on the vidilink. The President—a swell guy, fair and balanced—had also decamped from the campaign trail back to Washington while Eugene took his little breather on the beach.

With his spats crossed on top of the Oval Office desk, Bednap shot the breeze with Eugene: movies, current events, ass-banditry.

The Chancellor-President, his stentorian voice deep as a well, said through a yawn: "Don't know about you, but I'm about ready to get this turd hunt over and done with."

"Same here. What a drag this all is."

"I got me a spread down in Paraguay that needs its golf course broken in."

Eugene traced a finger in the fine white sand, which had been shipped in via cargo container. "I'm whipped. Four or eight years of chilling is what I'm looking forward to."

Bednap chuckled. "My boy—you're going to have a load of crap to clean up."

"No worries. My people will handle it."

"Hope they're better than mine." Bednap adopted a nonchalant air. "Ready for the debate?"

"Not really. When's the rehearsal?"

Bednap leaned out of the frame and shouted at an aide. Eugene heard a shuffling of papers and a muffled voice off camera.

The President came back and muttered, "Shit. Two weeks from today."

Sighing. "If we must."

"How's my girl?"

"Beatrice? Oh—she's fine. Keeping me in line."

"Good. You need a woman like her." Bednap's voice turned self-reflective. "We all do."

~

A MONTH LATER, Eugene announced to tumultuous acclaim that Beatrice would be his running mate.

Meanwhile, the lone fifteen-minute debate, its length dictated by law, unfolded mostly to script. Bednap turned the color of a rotting eggplant at the suggestion by Eugene that the administration's whole finding-oil-on-the-moon announcement had been a vile trick to justify making all the cars and trucks bigger again, but before the incumbent could retort, Eugene snapped off his boater and flung it at Bednap's throat like a Frisbee.

The President easily batted the hat away. He leaned in, winking at the moderator. "Now we'll see who's the real man around here."

The audience went apeshit as the President brandished a small plasma pistol, waving it around at Turtlechurch and the crowd, who screamed and ducked en masse.

In response, Eugene produced a vial of poisonous gas (a holographic effect courtesy of Industrial Light & Magic) and threw it at the stage between Bednap's spats. It broke with a sharp, cracking sound effect. A puff of green gas, snaking upward.

The audience lapsed into paroxysms of both joy and terror as Bednap launched into a well rehearsed approximation of imminent, chocking death, one from which he was saved at the last minute by Eugene's carefully prepared, ritualistic Native American dance of renewal and rebirth.

The throng, both in person and watching on their viewscreens, seemed dazzled by Eugene's balanced sense of equanimity and fair play, concepts foreign to most Americans; this passion play was meant to display, again, how Eugene Turtlechurch represented a new voice and a fresh start for a

country and a people who, by any objective standard, wallowed with helpless despair in abject stagnation.

ON THE WAY to the limos, President Bednap and President-to-be Turtlechurch engaged in a further faked fist-fight for the drone cameras following them, with the faux contretemps interrupted only after a woman in a dark veil slipped unseen through the security—it was as though she were a ghost—and blew a puff of purple vapor into the two candidate's faces. She vanished as soon as the smoke, no special effect this time, also did—into both candidates' flaring nostrils.

As every camera zoomed in, Turtlechurch's eyes spun like pinwheels. "Oh, lordy. It's concentrated essence of rabbit tobacco!" His innards groaned. "I need to find a bathroom!"

Bednap pirouetted in a circle declaring that the end of history had come upon the world; that the handlers were shape-shifting lizards who sought to terraform the earth into a dimensional plane more hospitable to their cold-blooded, slithering selves.

He again whipped out the pistol, but this time pointed it at his own face and actually fired; his head disappeared with a loud *POP* and left behind an acrid stench of burning mustache. The grievous wound cauterized, his headless, thick body pitched forward onto the concrete outside the auditorium like a sack of wet meat—which it was.

Eugene Turtlechurch, on the other hand, glowed as though struck by radioactive lightning. He raised his arms to the night sky, and the heels of his designer snakeskin cowboy boots rose a full six inches off the ground—he levitated in the newfound knowledge that he was free.

The words came tumbling out in a voice steady and true. "There is no *there* there, fellow babies, and now I will show you just how you can take back your freedoms and your lives by imagining a future apart from the one that's been crafted for you and implanted into your subconscious—I'm going to show you how to shift yourselves out of purgatory and back into the paradise this world was intended to be. Here's how it all really works—"

His words, forestalled by a flash of metal and a whipsaw snapping of his head: before Eugene could finish his pronouncement, Beatrice appeared out of nowhere and swung with practiced expertise at his tanned throat with a flaming, golden samurai sword. The measured stroke displayed to the world in that micro-moment how much Beatrice possessed prowess and discipline and rage and infinite knowledge.

Her husband's body, spurting thick blood—real blood—pitched forward. But the lenses stayed on Beatrice. The camera crews didn't even bother to shoot B-roll of Eugene Turtlechurch's death throes. Yesterday's papers.

Her hair ablaze, she cried out in triumph, in bloodlust; at last, t'was Beatrice who held the rapt attention of the entire planet.

Triumphal, she raised the sword in the air. As her own feet now rose from the asphalt—higher, much higher, than those of Eugene only moments before—the journalists and Secret Service agents and soldiers and other human beings knelt before her. Everyone could see the wires, which hung in plain sight, but no one seemed to mind.

The voices, in a single unified chant (actually a prerecorded track): "*Turtlechurch.*"

A chill and sudden wind blew in like an exhausted sigh from God. Nothing more needed to be said by the successor candidate, whose sword would continue to speak for her. An image rather than a person would rule; an object rather than a human being.

And it was thus that Beatrice Turtlechurch became the new leader of all the righteous peoples of the world, and it was to those same constituents her blade represented an assurance beyond belief, a force beyond reason, an occurrence of the godhead here and now among frail mortals. After the special effects crew pulled her out of the levitation rig, she took a congrat-ulatory call from Napthalia Sanganeer, an old pal who had been tapped to play the underdog in the big Girl-on-Girlfight of 2032, coming soon to a shimmering screen near you.

AUTHOR NOTE: After going through numerous drafts, titles, tones, and versions, this crude and crass political satire seemed destined to languish in the drawer as one of my 'early attempts,' but after the 2016 election season, the time seemed right to polish this up, give it one last title, and let it out into the world. Another wattpad.com entry.

LOCKED IN THE TRUNK OF A CAR

The rutted road. The dark. The smell of oily rags, the sloshing of the fuel in the tank. Hard edges, cramped, no comfort.

Panic turning to acceptance then rage; the will to fight back. To live.

Bumping along—miles to go, miles behind.

The trunk.

Trapped.

Destination?

Unknown.

Before: He stands mute, twinned by the mirror, raw, amorphous. He knows himself and yet not. Spinach, a clot in his teeth all night. Nobody told him. Brushing it away. Bitter paste. Stiff bristles. Bleeding gums.

Startled by movement, he sees the woman behind him—a reflection, asleep. She knows not of what lies inside him.

Of many things she knows not; not of the grand mistake, that which would be his undoing. The choice, the self subsumed.

Self.

Mind.

Unexposed, yet naked.

Consciousness fading, the pale light dimming in lavender-changing-to-black senescence.

Amber radiance blooms in the dark, click-click-click:

A turn signal.

The idle of the motor; a traffic light undermines free will, forces an interim. This he senses from the sound of cross traffic passing, panning left to right, right to left. Stereo.

Motion, returning. The crunch of gravel, stone crushed into grimy dust upon worn macadam.

Then: The smooth rush of the open road.

The thrum of the engine—modern, yet its force is measured, still, in the power of horses long dead.

Measures: of top speed, of distance gauged and traversed and remembered.

Three-tenths of a mile in mere seconds.

Beyond a certain velocity, survivability nil.

Forget the statistics. He knows this deep down in his fragile, chalky bones. Numbers. The first abstractions. From before the Fall.

A building looms: A tower of stone and glass; a lift of glass; glassed in on four sides and more still. Translucent; opaque; both at the same time. Layers and panels distorting from within and without.

A church, perhaps? From within which the mysteries of God might find explanation?

Neither; only his place of business, an office: an aquarium tank of cedar wood chips. A small mammal placed therein, aware only of hunger and thirst and fright. Lights overhead flickering at a rate designed to sap the will, deplete the nutrients, bleach the fabrics.

All eyes upon the rodent, trapped and ignorant of its own doom.

Expectations.

Requirements.

Purpose.

The reflection in the glass, the faces. The others, with their own private bag-lunches of bitter fruit.

In no better condition, them? Than the man in the trunk? But surely.

And again the next day.

Trapped.

Locked.

Inside.

A child—his progeny, a boy—speaking in its moment of quiet need.

The man knows, but the child does not.

Said; not said.

Consciousness growing before his lidded eyes; awareness.

The child, laughing with insouciance and grace. Silly old Daddy.

The child—a revelation. *The child.*

The child: A through-line.

A way out?

More than a boy—a lifebuoy.

The squealing of a worn brake pad. The murmur of voices, seen and unseen. A ticking stop watch. The momentary cooling of the horses. Journey's end, but not.

A pause; a low vibration.

Rumbling, throaty.

Motion.

Turn, turn, turn again.

The open road. Destination as yet unattained.

Airless, dark.

Out of the void. An old woman scented by camphor, lavender, disinfectant, sitting in a chair.

A windowless room.

A narrow bed.

An empty picture frame askew on the gray wall.

Eyes—hers. Large and wet, open.

Seeing all, seeing nothing.

Or else: what remains.

She knows, yet knows not.

Infinitude, looming. She doesn't give a rip, though. Ask her.

Smart girl, a voice whispers.

He sits beside her. Waits. When he says, "It's good to see you?" like a question, the old broad, she cackles. Says how it's good to be seen.

The man, he is of her, the woman, yet cannot fend for his intellect and its wonder at her impending absence. Worse, she remembers only on occasion that it is he—who he is—who sits before her on the chair across from the white linen of her resting bed.

He, however, is unable to forget. Would not want to.

He ponders. Speaks of her; thinks of himself. "How long?"

No one attending this woman, willing or otherwise, offers an answer. Amused, perhaps, by his uncertainty. The whole of their reply, ambiguous to a fault.

Comforted, he is not.

A booming, pulsing tone, as if from a great machine. Plangent, eternal. Floating back out of the nursing home, perceiving the facility a factory alive with endeavor. Feeding upon its workers.

A hive; a queen unseen.

This, all a hoax, a hallucination—the trunk the only space real. The only time; the only moment.

Quiet. A repast of silence. A doughnut would taste better.

The engine idling.

Stilling.

Ticking again into coolness. Into rest.

At peace.

Opening to the night air, a rush of cool and damp.

Rising.

Rise, old Lazarus! Rise!

Picturing: A field under starlight, a city in the distance on a hilltop, low cloud ceiling dyed ocher by the upward reflection of man-made light. The endless night, preceding lilac dawn.

Choices.

The trunk?

Or the day?

A memory of Home. A door; a leaf of green. Cherry oak popping in a fireplace. A spark, a cinder in an eye, the stab of hot pain.

Pain—but awake. And alive.

Outside, running. An endless field tangled with dry bitterweed. The breath in his throat clotted with the stink of wilting moonthorn, a hillside of sedge lying fallow and yellowed and dry-brittle.

The spins. Falling down.

A velvet sky of color-wheeling starlight, red-blue-green-white. Pinpoints of ice-crystal; hearts of fire. The seven sisters.

The source, the fount.

Another chance, if taken. Awaiting the day, would it deign to arrive.

Deteriorating frames from a film, a B-movie glimpsed late-night on a channel obscure, a story forgotten until remembered; consigned, again, to be forgotten.

A cycle.

A chain, unbroken.

The car, again; the journey ongoing. The slipping of the fan belt. A hole in a muffler. Acrid exhaust like stinging flatus—a byproduct of decay.

The trunk, opening. A clock, the green-glow numerals changing from one to another, inexorable. Execrable.

A sequence.

The morning. Of an ordinary day.

And not a trunk. Only lying beside his wife in a bed.

He thinks of himself. Of his mother, dying.

Of his spouse, and the child, he who is of them.

He imagines.

He feels, finally.

He pushes down the covers from his face, opens the lid of the trunk, just so—a crack of light. Peers out.

Outside of the trunk.
Outside of himself.
Sun, cresting a hillside xanthous and dusty.
Quotidian.
Yet not.
And now, as before: He waits. For the ride in the trunk to be over; for the ride to begin. The ride.

AUTHOR NOTE: As experimental a piece as I have ever written, this spare but lush glimpse into a workaday family man's dreamscape was first written in a few minutes while hurtling through the air to NYC on a jet aircraft, three or four pages of free writing that isn't substantially different from what is presented here. What was on my mind that day with all this? Too many years have elapsed. Never before published.

RUBY IN THE DUST

R uby made a call to Hiram Fant, an old family friend, someone glad to hear from her. The next day he drove over to look at her truck, which she hated to sell so bad it was about to make her sick.

But money, which everyone always needed, now felt critical on a whole n'other level. She felt change wafting on the wind, like the smell of the offal from the chicken farm up the road. Knew money was gonna come in handy. Like it always did.

Much as she could get together.

If she had the guts to make a move, finally.

Had enough of Willie Lowdown's hot mess. Willie Lowdown —her little nickname for Rennie DeBruhl, her man. If you could call him that. Everybody kept telling her he'd never change for the better.

He used to be sweet to her. Wait—that was the problem. He'd already changed.

Standing around the pickup truck in the sandy back yard amidst skinny pine trees, the dog in the house barked like he was losing his mind. Brownie, an excitable little mutt she'd found on the side of the road last year, had to be put away to keep from jumping onto Mr. Fant's khaki pants.

Mr. Fant hooked thick thumbs into a wide belt beneath his old man's belly, one earned over the course of a well-fed life. His face had deep lines, but he still had a young air about him; a twinkle glimmered in wise old eyes. "Didn't think you'd ever consider selling Big Chief."

"You know how the times is."

"God-*daw*-mighty if I don't. Hard to make a living anymore."

"You mean an honest living?"

"Honey—I'm in the car business." Winking. "Honest as the day is long."

She scoffed. Knew how much "honest" money that old fart had. More than almost anyone else in town.

Ruby, however, hadn't worked for quite a spell, not since Jeanette's Nursery closed down after forty years selling plants and pottery and gardening tools folks now bought from Tractor Supply or Home Depot. "Keeping this old truck up ain't getting me nowhere, that's for sure."

"Never thought I'd see the day." His eyes, blue as ever, stared her down. But he didn't look Ruby over the way most men did—fifty or not, she still had that sparkle and wiggle in her walk. Fant had known her daddy and granddaddy. Like an uncle to her. "You sure about this?"

"I called, didn't I?"

Mr. Fant ambled over and rested his freckled hand on the front fender. Took off his straw cowboy hat, ran a handkerchief over his pate, belched grease from his lunch. He had been dealing cars for as long as Ruby could remember. Had been the mayor. Had done this'n that. Knew everyone. Knew everything going on. He was a Master Craftsman at the Masonic lodge, whatever that meant. "Don't make them solid like this no more."

"Ain't the point. What do I need two cars for?" Two years ago he had found her a high-mileage Outback in which she ran around, a good solid car. "Don't nobody need to pay taxes and insurance on a car they don't drive."

"C'ain't argue with that."

"Sits right where you see it, except when Rennie runs over to the dump." To herself. "When he takes a notion."

Faraway. "A good truck. We sold a good number of them, back in the day."

"I remember when Poppa brung Big Chief home—brand new, right off the lot."

Fant came back to the here and now. "That Subaru, she holding up?"

"I keep it up good."

"Like your daddy taught you."

Brownie stopped barking, finally. "Damn straight."

In any case, the Outback made for a more economical vehicle than Big Chief. Lord, but the gas mileage on that mother, an '87 GMC Classic Sierra K10, gray on blue with the red-stripe detailing. When you cranked her up, she roared like a beast.

No—Ruby couldn't see taking Big Chief with her. Not where she was going.

The mountains.

That Outback, which she got for a song after trading Mr. Fant her Ford Taurus, wasn't a car—it was a lifeboat. This latest mess with Rennie wasn't no recent thing, and the woman this time? Young.

And while Ruby wasn't getting any younger, time had come to get out of his hick flatland where she'd come up. She had half a life left to live. Her granny, who died in the nursing home last year, had made it to ninety-eight.

Yeah—see? Ruby had herself a plan underway. No more if's about it. That'd been why she wanted the Outback, because of the all-wheel drive. When she finally left Rennie and moved up to Asheville, which she had been dreaming about doing for a coon's age, she would need a car like that.

But that was two years ago now, when she first decided to move up yonder.

Mercy.

Life got in the way. For a whole year Ruby had ended up

running that wagon more than a New York taxi cab but had yet to get anywhere, not during the spell when she had had to look after her sister's young'uns. They lived all the way on the other side of Columbia, almost to Orangeburg. Had put as many miles on that wagon as the Earth was round. But still stuck here in Edgewater County.

At least her sister's cancer had gotten better instead of finishing her off, thank the Lord. Lynn said she didn't know what was worse: the cancer, or the chemo they give her to get rid of the disease. But those kids of her'n, they were the hellions to beat all. Ruby was lucky—she could just as soon have them on her hands now, as well her overgrown child of a man. Wouldn't that be a mess.

Mr. Fant grunted and spat juice into the dirt. Announced what he'd give for the GMC.

Ruby just about shit. It was too much. "Well now, that ain't a fair price."

"Says who?"

She reminded Mr. Fant of the condition of the valves she'd been planning to get to fixing later in the year—maybe even get Cody Jarnow to help her drop and rebuild the whole engine. Ruby, good with cars. Knew her stuff.

"Girl, you think I don't know what a truck like that's worth? I been in the car business since it was still horse and buggy." That was bullcrud, of course. "Shoot."

"Ain't the same truck you sold my Poppa. That's all I know."

Mr. Fant's round, stooped shoulders gave a shrug, but only a teensy bit. He changed the subject. Pointed. "Y'all got mold growing up yonder on the siding."

"No duh."

"That Rennie, he ain't took care of this house worth a durn."

"I should've made him marry me. Maybe he'd've took better care of it."

Another stream of brown juice. "Woulda-shoulda-coulda. If that boy's daddy was still alive, he'd whip his butt."

She stood her ground. "I can't take that much for Big Chief."

He snorted like a mean, mad bull, but Ruby knew Hiram Fant wasn't nothing but an old softie. "A good clean GMC like this? It's worth something."

"'Clean'—that's a good one. Mighty sweet of you. Ain't a bit of rust on it, though. I'll say that much."

"You'd be surprised how much life one of these old trucks still has, long as you still got a sturdy frame."

She leaned against Big Chief. "Like you said—this was back when they still made 'em good."

"That's the god's truth right there."

Ruby remembered Mr. Fant and her Poppa drinking beer in the front yard and cackling like the old friends they were, even back then. They had been fellow businessmen here in Edgewater County. Mendenhall Landscaping, Fant Motors. A pair of town fathers.

No wonder he wanted to give her the money—once Poppa passed away, Mr. Fant had promised he was gonna look after her. Her daddy, like so many around here, took sick with his own cancer. What a time that was—near the end, after Poppa had started puking up black like he was slap-full of death, she and Lynn had had to change and wash his bedclothes three times a day. Ruby, dutiful.

Like she still was with her no-good man. Washing his drawers that come home smelling like another woman's body. It was just what you done, she reckoned. You done what you had to do for you and your'n.

Except it was time she did for herself for real. For once.

She gave Mr. Fant a hug. "The Mendenhall girls always appreciated our favorite uncle."

He grinned. "That's more like it. I'm gonna go by the bank and get you a check cut. I'll drop off Rusty later on to pick up Big Chief." His blonde eyebrows wiggled. "It will drive, won't it?"

"What you talking about? Of course it'll drive." She looked

over at the old GMC pickup truck. Ruby's voice broke. "I'll—draw up a bill of sale."

He shook his head, said *naw*. "Who's in the car business? You, or me?"

"Neither one, last time I checked."

"That's about the truth." Mr. Fant's son ran the car and mobile home lot now. At least it was still open for business. "But it stays in the blood."

"That's why I called you."

"You know I'll always be here for you."

That was a laugh. No one would always be there. But still a sweet thing to say.

Watching Mr. Fant shuffle around front, she called after him to shut the gate so she could let out Brownie, who was liable by now to have messed in the kitchen.

Ruby got a cold knot in her stomach—was leaving gonna work after all?

What would she say to Rennie when he got home later?

Would he even notice the truck gone?

Probably not until tomorrow. He hadn't said a word about how busy she had been around the house, cleaning out old clothes. Putting things into boxes. The house was full of junk from all the years his folks lived there, none of which she'd be taking with her. Had always been after him to clean it all out, but you know Rennie: always another beer to drink, or a race to watch on TV.

Ruby wasn't kidding around no more—her friend April said she could get her a job in Hot Springs, tucked way back in them mountains up in North Carolina.

As the little brown dog jumped up onto her jeans, it struck her: Big Chief turned out to be her escape vehicle after all, in his way. She wasn't gonna miss much around here. But she was gonna miss that truck.

Especially after she decided to take the Outback to the store to get pork chops to cook for Rennie's supper, a good last supper for him so he'd remember what she had meant to his life. Damn if the engine wouldn't turn over—she discovered that the hatch hadn't been closed good, and the dome light inside had run down the battery.

Ruby stood in the dusty front yard with her hands on her hips, waved to the mailman dropping off circulars and junk. Shit. Now she'd have to buy a battery. Spending money she hadn't even gotten her hot hands on yet. If that wasn't her luck, she'd like to know what was.

AUTHOR NOTE: Appearing in the 2017 edition of premiere South Carolina literary magazine **Fall Lines**, *this Edgewater County entry represents the most recent work in this volume, and certainly of a piece with the rest of my short fiction in setting, character, and theme. Written in late 2016, here's hoping Ruby Mendenhall got that battery and made it to the mountains.*

James D. McCallister is the author of four novels and numerous shorter pieces of fiction and creative nonfiction. A lifelong South Carolinian, he lives in West Columbia with his wife and beloved brood of cats, muses all.

For more information:

www.jamesdmccallister.com
editor@mindharvestpress.com

ALSO BY JAMES D. MCCALLISTER

King's Highway

Fellow Traveler

Let the Glory Pass Away

Dogs of Parsons Hollow (2018)

MHP

Mind Harvest Press
COLUMBIA, SC